man IN UNIFORM

HE'S ON THE CASE... **AND IN HER HEART.**

CASSIE MAE

Man in Uniform
Published by Cassie Mae
Cassiemaeauthor.com
Cover Design: Y'all That Graphic
Editing: CookieLynn Publishing Services
Formatting: CookieLynn Publishing Services

man
IN
UNIFORM

Dedicated to The Wounded Warriors. Thank you for all you do.

chapter one

Hazel

There's a Coke Slurpee stain the size of the sun on my left boob.

"Crap on a cracker," I mutter under my breath, swiping at the thing, but I'm only making it a thousand times worse… and getting it all over my seatbelt. I knew I should've sucked the overflow while I was standing in the 7-Eleven, but I was in a hurry.

I ease to a stop at the light, pulling my shirt from my body and wrinkling my nose at the giant brown stain on my white top. Great, now I've got rock tit from the icy drink, and I'll have to change before I log onto the stream. I once started a five-hour stream in a crocheted number my mom made me for Christmas. The thing was unbelievably comfortable, and I wanted to be festive for the holidays. I clicked on the stream and started playing hours upon hours of League of Legends, and when I finally looked at chat, it was full of emotes that were telling me my nipple was poking out of one of the holes in my sweater.

I wish I could say that's the most embarrassing thing that's happened to me, but it doesn't even crack the top ten.

Someone honks, and I stop swiping at my Slurpee mess, give them an apology wave, and step on the gas. It's a lost cause—trying to make this stain any better—so I grab my drink and take a sip. It's not long before I get to the point when I have to stir the ice around so I can actually sip something up the straw, but since I'm driving, I shake the cup instead to loosen things up.

The lid pops off in my hand, and the cup plummets to my lap, soaking my leg in Coke and ice.

"Shit, nononononono…" I squeal, trying to keep one eye on the road while scooping ice back into the cup. A whoop of a siren goes off, and red and blue light up my rearview.

"Ugh," I groan, pulling to the side of the road. The cop probably thinks I'm drunk, but really, I'm a klutz.

My heart thuds in my Slurpee covered chest, and I breathe out, hoping my face looks innocent, but I've never been good at poker. The cop steps out, donning a gray polo under his vest, his badge hooked to the upper left strap. He's in an unmarked car, and I wonder if he's been following me since the gas station. He might've been the honker when I wasn't moving at the green light back there.

When he gets to my trunk, I roll down my window, letting the autumn air blast in and whip the frays from my messy bun away from my face. I put on a cheesy grin for when he finally leans down to talk to me.

"Hey there," he says, and when he bends, an unholy, involuntary noise that sounds like the spawn of a cow and a demon escapes my lips. Sweet, ever-loving Jesus, this man has the most gorgeous eyes in all the universe. Green, but not hazel green or emerald green. Seagreen. Gorgeous green. My favorite color green. And when I get enough strength to tear my gaze away from that green, I get a good hard look at the rest of his face. That sweet jawline, the curly brown locks pushed back by a pair of sunglasses, bushy brows, and the slightest bit of stubble. My jaw slacks, and I stare like a dead fish on a hot beach, gasping for anything to quench my sudden thirst.

I take back every fantasy I've had about men. Sorry Chris Pratt, you've just been dethroned.

He tilts his head. "Are you okay, ma'am?"

Ma'am? How deep are the bags under my eyes today? "Uh… oh… um… yep!"

That bushy brow lifts, and I internally slap my forehead. I have never been one to lose coherency over a sexy man, but then again, I haven't seen one in a while. Most guys I interact with are virtual, and their avatars are ogres or wizards.

"Do you know why I pulled you over?"

"Oh, probably because of my drinking problem." I snort, but since I'm the only one in on my clever joke, he doesn't crack even the slightest of grins.

"Will you step out for me?" he asks, moving away from the door.

I blow out a sigh, slumping my hand on the handle and pushing the door open. Leave it to me to make all situations worse. I stand up, and the chunks of Slurpee I didn't manage to clean up slop to the asphalt. He watches it, and the first sign he has a sense of humor shows in the corner of his mouth.

"I'm not drunk," I blurt, raising my hands in the air. "I spilled my Slurpee on my boob, then it dumped on my lap. I'm just a hot mess with a driver's license."

He doesn't move, doesn't flinch. Just stares with those hypnotizing seagreen eyes. I bet he's brilliant at poker.

"You can put your hands down," he says, nodding slightly at my raised arms. Heat blossoms in my cheeks as I let my arms fall, my right hand slapping the wet part of my red and blue plaid pajama pants.

"Sorry," I mumble, unsure of what I'm apologizing for. Maybe just all of me.

He crosses his arms. "You veered into the left lane for a good ten seconds before swerving into the bike lane here on the right. Did you notice?"

I shake my head. "I was a little distracted."

"No kidding."

Oh my gosh, a joke. This man can joke. I let out

another so attractive snort, and the amusement in the corner of his mouth reaches his eyes.

Gah, those eyes. They are even better when they are smiling.

"Do you have your license and registration?"

"Oh, yeah." I hurry and reach inside the car, grappling around for the papers and shuffling things in my tote bag for my license. When I reemerge, he has his hand resting on the gun on his hip. Oh… I probably shouldn't have dove in for my records like that.

I hand my registration over slowly, almost like I do when I approach my cat when he doesn't want to be touched and I want all the snuggles. He takes it from my outstretched hand, and I zone out on the veins in his forearms for longer than I should.

"You can have a seat in your car." He waits till I'm back inside, sitting in soaked Coke Slurpee, before making his way to his own driver's seat. I tap my hands on the wheel, my heart still thump, thump, thumping. I've been pulled over a few times in the ten years since I got my license, but never got a ticket. I'm the queen of warnings. Once I got a written one when I was at GamerCon. I framed it, and it's currently in my background shot, right next to my million-subscriber plaque.

After a good five minutes—and finishing the piddly remains of my Slurpee—he walks up to my window, and I promise not to look at those eyes so I can form a proper sentence.

"Okay, I've given you a citation for failure to maintain a lane. You'll call this number here at the bottom to pay the fine, and my name and badge number for your reference. You have ninety days to get this taken care of."

I blink a few times, staring at the thing in his hand. A ticket. My first ticket.

"Do you have any questions?"

"Can I frame it?" I blurt. I wish my mouth would wait for my brain before it pops off.

A low laugh meets my ears, and I whip my head so fast my neck cracks.

Officer Stoic is smiling. Laughing. At me. At my joke. And it is heavenly. Good job, mouth. You keep that shit up.

"Whatever you want to do with this ticket is your prerogative." His laughter fades away, but that smile stays in place. "Just keep your car in your lane from now on, yeah? Maybe pull over if you have any more… drinking problems."

"You got it." I take my stuff, including the ticket. He wishes me a safe drive home, and I watch his ass as he makes his way to his car. If he's going to give me a ticket and never see me again, I reserve the right to ogle.

I pull out carefully, pretending I'm playing Mario Kart and I have to stay in the lines all the way to my house. I bought the three-bedroom, two bathroom as a divorce present to myself a little over a year ago. Divorce wasn't awesome, and it's not like I made out with much in it, but I hit it big in the gaming world and was able to apply for the loan all on my own. I like to joke that I'm the unluckiest person on the planet, but the way I fell into my career was all luck. If that's the only thing I get, I'll take it.

I park in the garage and let the door close behind me as I go in through the kitchen. Cheeto meows at me from his bowl. Heaven forbid he sees the bottom of it. I pick it up and shake it so the food covers the blue plastic and set it down. He's satisfied with that maneuver and dives in for dinner.

"Silly boy," I tell him, ripping off my stained shirt. I pour a glob of detergent on the stain, take off my pajama bottoms, and do the same to it, then toss them in the washer. Since that's done, I may as well find out how much I owe the government for my mishap. I wrinkle my nose at the yellow paper. It's not as entertaining now without a sexy guy hand delivering it to me. A pile of rusty nerves grows in my stomach while I research ticket fines for the state of Utah.

"Detective Stoll," I muse, my eyes drifting over his name. "Detective, huh? Didn't know you guys did the traffic stop thing." I guess if the person in front of him is all over the road, he has to. Explains the unmarked car, though.

I click through and scroll, and when I spot the failure to maintain a lane fine, my hand slaps against the counter, scaring Cheeto out of the room. "A hundred and fifty bucks? You're kidding me!"

I mutter some expletives under my breath and vow to never have Coke Slurpees behind the wheel again. What an expensive dinner break.

I clench my teeth and march to my room to put on my back-up pajamas. At least I have one hell of a story to tell my chat during this next stream.

I redo my messy bun and trudge on over to my gaming room. When I moved in, I had it set up professionally because I needed to be serious about this stuff. I got it soundproofed, and the background is aesthetically pleasing, and my pride and joy—my computer—has three monitors, a seagreen backlit keyboard, and stations for my mic, my headphones, and a mini fridge. It's the best place in the world—if I don't count online as a place.

Cheeto paws at the door, and I tell him to be patient. He's allowed in here only because my chat loves him to death. He's the orange chonk that occasionally steps on my keyboard and blows my entire game. And my viewers love that.

I step in, flicking on my LEDs for the back light, keeping my eyes on Cheeto. He likes to bite my cords, and I have to grab him before he takes off. For a big guy, he's fast. I snatch him before he gets far, gather him in my arms, patting his head, and slump into my green gamer chair. "All right… let's get star—"

My voice sucks into my throat, and my heart plummets straight out of my ass.

Everything—my computer, monitors, keyboard, mouse, mic—all of it, is gone.

chapter two

Hunter

I rub my eyes, leaning my head against the headrest. Traffic stops are my least favorite things to do on the job, and I avoid them most times, but that girl was all over the place. I honestly thought she needed medical attention. When it turned out to be nothing but a spilled drink, I ended up laughing in my car for a good five minutes before heading home.

I didn't get twenty minutes before dispatch called me. Guess there was a burglary, and as the guy who's on call for property crimes this week, I'm the one who's gotta head out there.

Property isn't exactly the department I wanted when I was asked to move to detectives, but my affinity for finding stolen vehicles while I was on patrol led me to where I am now. I hope to move to major crimes, but I'm paying my dues. Patrol was a lot more action packed, a lot more fulfilling. Property, unfortunately, involves me taking down information and reassuring the victim, but nine times out of ten, they ain't seeing their stuff again.

One day, I'd like to actually make a difference with this badge.

I hit my lights and pull out of my drive. The address is fifteen minutes into the city, so I have a bit of a ways to go, living at the base of the mountain. My phone rings, and I have Bluetooth pick it up.

"Detective Stoll."

"Hey. You need me to go to the burg?"

Weir. He's my property buddy. We've been in the same department for five years now.

"Nah, I'm on my way. I closed out a case earlier, so I've got room on my plate for it anyhow."

"You sure? I'm close."

"I'm sure…" I drag it out, confusion piling in me. Weir doesn't often offer to take stuff off my hands. He knows I like the work.

"All right," he says. "Let me know if you want backup."

"Got it."

The beep of a dropped call rings through the cab, and I turn up the Koffin Kats and jam out to them the rest of the trip.

I arrive at a house in the South Salt Lake suburbs,

leaving my lights on. I nod to patrol, who is already here, securing the scene. He nods back, and I make my way up the walk.

The door is a bright yellow, standing out from the neighbors' blue and brown doors. Brown and red leaves fall from the maple tree blocking the house, covering the yellowing grass. The roots have taken over the sidewalk path, the cement cracking and lifting from the force of growth.

A kid about ten or eleven waves from across the street, and I wave back with a friendly grin. Any chance I can encourage kids to not be afraid of cops, I do it.

The door swings open, and my brows lift at the familiar face staring back at me.

"You're kidding me." Her shoulders slump under an oversized maroon hoodie, the words Dragon Slayer splayed across the chest. I see she's changed out of the Coke covered clothing that allowed me to see a little too much of that pink bra she donned. I wonder if she's still wearing that for a split second before remembering I'm on the job.

"Hello there, Hazel Bardot," I say, hooking my thumbs into my belt. "Not having the best day, are we?"

Her bottom lip juts out, and if that isn't the damn cutest thing I've ever seen, I'll eat my badge. "They took my computer."

I try to erase my amusement at her sweet pout and put on my business face. "Can I take a look?"

She pulls the yellow door all the way open, standing

back and waving me forward. An orange ball of fur hisses at me from the corner of her living room.

"Knock it off, Cheeto." She tilts her head, gesturing to me to follow. I take a wide berth around the cat and follow her to a room just set off from a small dining area. Girl is doing pretty well for herself, considering her age.

"In here. They took everything."

I step into a cooler room, black foam covering one of the walls, LED lights attached where the walls meet the ceiling. A light ring sits in the corner, and a long, wooden desk with dust marks takes up the entire back wall. Other than a few stray cords, it's empty.

I pull my phone out. "I need to take some photos."

"Do your thing, Detective." She waves me forward, slumping against the wall. "They didn't touch a single thing in my house except my gaming stuff. It's like they found this room, said 'JACKPOT!' and left."

I nod, jotting that away. "Was it just your computer?"

"My tower, three monitors, keyboard…" she starts, ticking them off on her fingers. "My Xbox, Playstation, Switch. All the games I own that aren't virtual and all my controllers. My mic, headphones, back-up headphones, my back-up back-up headphones… pretty much everything I use for my job."

She's a YouTuber. I don't know why that amuses me, but my lips twitch, and I can't help but grin when she's not looking. "You sure there wasn't anything else taken?"

"I don't have anything else. My bread and butter are in this room." Her voice starts to shake, and I glance over my shoulder. Her eyes lift to the ceiling, a watery wall filling them. A piece of her blonde hair falls from her bun, and she fills her cheeks with air, letting it seep out in wisps.

Normally I'd ask her more questions… when she thinks it happened, if she has cameras on the house, if there is anyone who might have done this, if she's talked to any of the neighbors. And I'll get to that. But the urge to reassure her pulls at me unexpectedly. I don't know if it's guilt for giving her a ticket earlier or if it's just that she looks so defeated, but I take off my job hat for a minute and put on a human one.

"I'm so sorry about this, Hazel. I'm going to do everything I can to get your stuff back."

She lets out a snort, swiping under her eye before a tear falls. "No offense, and it's nothing against your ability to do your job, but I know how this goes. You'll check a pawnshop, find out it's already been sold, and I'm SOL. I'll have to call home insurance to get money for a new setup, which they will severely underestimate in terms of how much it's worth, and I'll dump my entire savings into replenishing what took me years to build."

"Wow," I say, lifting some prints from her desk chair. "Someone's a ray of sunshine." Or been through this before.

"Oh, I'm sorry. Am I supposed to be happy I got robbed after getting a hundred and fifty dollar ticket?"

My mouth pulls in apology, and I manage to get a small smile out of her before she shakes her head.

"I don't know what I'm going to do without my stuff."

I tuck my phone into my pocket. "I know you have your doubts, but I am going to do my best." I am. I will. "In the meantime, I might have something that can help."

"Do you have a timeturner?"

"A Harry Potter reference. I like it."

"I like that you recognize it." She tucks her hands into her front hoodie pocket, a slight blush covering her cheeks, matching the color of pink reflecting off a subscriber plaque. It's no wonder she's popular online. She's the cutest person I've met.

"It's not much, but if you need a computer, I have an extra laptop. I don't mind if you borrow it until I recover the one that was stolen."

She straightens. "You just have a computer lying around?"

"It's probably not as fancy as yours, but it works. I just got a new one."

Her eyes narrow. "How old is this laptop?"

"Couple years."

"And you got a new one because…?"

"Felt like it." And I wanted a ten-key, and my laptop didn't have one.

She studies me, like she wants to know what I'm not saying, but I keep my face passive.

"So…" I prod after a minute. "You want to borrow it?"

Her tongue snakes out and wets her lips. "I suppose beggars can't be choosers."

"I'll take that as a yes." I take my pen from my pocket and my small notepad. "And while we're at it, can I ask you a few questions?"

"Fire away." Her eyes widen, her mouth forming a circle. "I mean with your questions. Not your gun."

A laugh jumps from the back of my throat. "Yeah, I didn't think you wanted me to shoot you."

* * *

I slump into my trusty chair in the living room at my brother Miles' place. I've plopped into it so much that it's got my ass groove in the cushion and groans when I kick my boots off. Immediately after leaving Hazel's, I went straight to the pawnshop, like she predicted I would. Surprisingly, they didn't have anybody come in with the stuff I described. Not only did they not, but the next five pawn shops I hit after didn't either. It's nearing three a.m., and I know I could've gone home right after writing up the report, but I don't know… I was hoping for a win, and by the time I stopped, Miles' place was closer, and I need sleep.

Not only that, but… I have a tendency to be "overbearing" as my siblings call it. And three out of my four siblings live under this roof. With the robbery fresh in my mind, the urge to check on them was too strong.

All three are sleeping soundly, and I'm put at ease for

the time being.

Hershey, my brother's chocolate lab, sets her head on my knee, and I give her the scratches she's begging for. "Hey, girl," I grunt out, exhaustion taking over. She puts her paw up on my leg, and even though she's eighty pounds, I pat my thigh, and she jumps into my lap. Her cold, wet nose pushes at my chin, and I let out a tired laugh.

"Yeah, it was a long day. Got hung up on a case." Hazel's sad eyes flash through my mind. Her eyes match her name. They were big and bright, fitting perfectly with her round features. She seems so… innocent. And my jaded ass can't comprehend it, but I also want to defend it.

I scratch under Hershey's arm, letting my mind wander. I gave the pawnshops my number and asked them to call if anything came in. I'll talk to Hazel's neighbors tomorrow… see if they saw anything. I'll be dropping off my laptop at her place, anyway.

"Shit," I mutter, running a hand over my forehead. I don't know what possessed me to offer my personal laptop. I don't know if I'm allowed with a victim of an active case, but I sure as hell know I'm toeing some sort of line. Maybe Sarg will go easy on me… if he ever finds out.

Hershey gets settled, her weight pulling me into a different kind of exhaustion. I doze off to visions of Hazel when I recover her stuff, that awkward smile and adorable blush sinking into my dreams.

chapter three

Hazel

"So, that's why I haven't been streaming. Sorry I couldn't tell you all sooner, but thank you so much for sticking around! I promise once I get a new computer or—God willing—my computer back, I'll bring you lots more content. Until then…" I pick up Cheeto and put him on my lap in view of the camera. I hold his paw and move it up and down in a wave. "Bye-bye, awesome humans."

I end the video and start uploading it. Since my longass story of how I was robbed while getting a ticket was nearly an hour with all the flair and drama I put into telling it, and Detective Stoll's laptop is super slow, I figure it's going to take more than the typical twenty minutes it usually does to post.

I push from my very sad, very empty desk. Cheeto plops from my lap to the floor. I could use a Coke Slurpee right about now. I'm not ashamed to say I have an addiction, and it's not like I got to drink a lot of the last one I treated myself to.

After grabbing my keys and tucking my feet into my slippers, I head out, making sure to stay in my lane the whole way to 7-Eleven.

Margie, the gal behind the counter, gives me a hello and wave as the bell rings above me. Most of the people here know me. Not by name, but by face. The manager will sometimes waive the dollar-seven for my Slurpee, and I get a freebie for the day. Those are the best.

I pull the blue cup from its holder and push the curved lid into place. Sad… the Coke isn't ready yet, so I move to my second drug of choice—the Mountain Dew. I bop to the music overhead, celebrating that if I can't have my computer, at least I have Slurpees.

"You sure that's the best idea?" a low voice asks from over my shoulder. I jump, spilling the ice cold slush all over my hand. Detective Stoll laughs, reaching over my head for a napkin.

"Slurpees are always a good idea," I stumble through a staccato laugh. Our hands brush as I take the napkin, and my heart shorts out. "I'll make sure I keep it in the cup holder until I make it home this time."

"Responsible drinking. Seems you've learned your lesson." He smiles, and my knees wobble, making it that much harder to put the straw into the hole at the top of the lid. He most likely knows the effect he has on me, but I'm not sure if he knows the reason. Hell, I don't even know if my fumbling is because he's a cop or because he's a sexy cop.

My gaze drops down his tall frame, and I take a casual sip of my Slurpee. The sweet taste of Mountain Dew surprises me for a moment. I'm so used to Coke.

"Are you on duty, Detective?" I ask, nodding to his tan cargos and navy t-shirt. He's sans badge, but that could be on his belt.

"Not yet." He nods to my slippers. "Are you?"

"Just taking a break." I give him a cheesy grin and kick my leg up to show off my fuzzy footwear.

He grins, like he enjoys my quirks, then juts his thumb to the Slurpee machine. "I've had a craving for one since I pulled you over."

"Well, they're out of the best kind," I tell him with a pout.

"What'd you recommend as a substitute?"

I hold my drink up, showing him the green slush. "Mountain Dew… but for the caffeine, not the taste." I turn to the machines, pointing at the options. "If you don't mind a mad sugar rush, the wild cherry is good. Sometimes I mix it with Coke and it's…" I blow a chef's kiss, and he chuckles—it's the best sound in the entire universe.

"A real Slurpee Connoisseur. Looks like I came at the right time." He pulls the green cup out, choosing the medium size over my small. He sets it under the Mountain

Dew, and I grab his arm.

"Don't pour it yet!"

He clutches at his chest. "Jesus, you scared the hell out of me."

"Sorry," I say through a laugh, reaching for a lid. "But put the lid on first and pour through the hole."

He lifts an eyebrow, and I get lost in those sea green eyes for a split second. "Is that a rule or something I don't know about?"

"Is this your first Slurpee in your life?" I rest my butt on the counter, toying with the straw between my teeth. "Amateur."

He shakes his head, amusement tickling the corners of his mouth, but he puts the lid on and dispenses his Slurpee out correctly. The green slush slops into the cup until he stops it where the lid meets the edge, then he moves to the cherry and tops it off. Hmm, I haven't tried cherry Mountain Dew, but I'll put it on the list for the future.

"So, how's that laptop working out for you?" he asks, unwrapping a spoon straw.

"Fine, I guess. I can't stream with it, because it's so slow. I think it's all that porn I found on there."

He chokes on his first sip, and I back up to avoid the spray, grabbing him a napkin. "Uh… if there's porn, it wasn't mine."

"Sure," I tease, handing the napkin over. "And the background picture… that isn't you either?"

The corner of his mouth lifts. "No, I'll take credit for that."

"Really?" I make a face. "I wouldn't."

"That was a brook trout. Gorgeous fish."

"And it was what? Three inches long?" I wrinkle my nose playfully.

"At least four." He chucks his napkin into the garbage. "You snoop through anything else?"

"You worried, Detective?"

"Not sure yet. Honestly, I have no idea what I left on that laptop."

"Sadly, not a lot."

"Just the porn."

"Earmuff porn."

"Excuse me?"

I point to my ears. "Just lots of women in nothing but earmuffs."

He laughs, and I'm so happy he enjoys my sense of humor that my mouth decides to spout off again without my brain's permission.

"I like your laugh," I blurt, and his laughter somewhat dies, his brow furrowing from the unexpected compliment. Is it a compliment? Or is it just weird?

"I like yours, too."

"Shut up. I have the world's least attractive laugh. Like a pig choking on its tongue."

"It's adorable." And as he says it, the tops of his ears burn bright red. My darn knees wobble something fierce, and I completely miss my mouth with the straw, jabbing myself in the cheek.

"W-well," I stutter, "I'd say I need to run into you more often for a boost in my ego, but you're only one for three."

"Meaning?"

"The first time, I got a ticket. The second, I cried over my missing stuff."

He purses his lips, his amazing jaw flexing. "Guess I'll have to improve my stats. Recover your things for you."

"I mean, if you could…" I give him another cheesy grin, which he finds hilarious, and I vow to be as dorky as possible around him if I keep getting these reactions.

My phone buzzes in my pocket, and I let out an "oh!" and check the caller ID. "Sorry, quick second." He nods, assuring me silently he's not going anywhere, and I answer my ex-husband's call. "Hello?"

"Hey. I just saw your video. Are you all right?"

Guess my thing uploaded. He, for sure, hasn't watched it all yet; probably has it paused in the background. Leave it to Kevin to click on his notifications the second they pop up.

"I'm okay. Pissed I can't do my work, but hopefully the cops will find something."

"You got them looking?"

"I'm staring the detective in the face this very second." I wink at Detective Stoll, and I'm rewarded with those red ears again.

"Let me know if you need anything."

"I will. Thanks."

"Yep. Stay safe."

We say our goodbyes, and I apologize again. "Sorry. My ex just found out about the burglary and was just checking in."

His eyes widen. "You're close with your ex?"

"It was a pretty amicable divorce, as far as divorces go." An awkward silence spreads over us, and I bite my bottom lip, unsure of what to say.

"Sorry. Divorce is rough, even when it's amicable."

"Thanks." I take a sip from my melting Slurpee. "You divorced, too?"

"No. Never been married. But my parents went through it."

A sympathetic frown pulls my lips. "How old were you when they split?"

"Twenty-two. They wanted to wait for all us kids to get out of the house, but they didn't quite make it."

"How many siblings do you have?"

"Four. Two brothers, two sisters. My youngest sister was fourteen."

"And where do you land? Wait! Let me guess…" I hold up a finger, and he sits back and lets me think. "Oldest."

A mix of surprise and shyness cross his expression. "Is it obvious?"

I lift a shoulder. "A little. You have this protective nature around you, but that could be because of your career."

"I suppose that's why I got into it, yes."

"You like it?"

He presses his lips together again, and I watch him consider the question, that jaw ticking, and I like that I already know his thinking face.

"Yes."

I lift a brow. "Hmm."

"What?"

"You don't sound very convincing, but I'll believe you."

We start making our way to the register, and my heart thuds hard in my chest. I don't want to stop talking to him. I get maybe three minutes a week of IRL conversation, and I didn't realize how much I like it. Or maybe I just like it with him. It's a tossup.

"That'll be one-o-seven," Margie tells me, and I give her exact change from the pocket in my slouchy pants. Since I don't carry a purse, and my wardrobe comprises loungewear, I made sure to only buy comfy pants with pockets—which are sadly a rare find.

I move over and wait for Detective Stoll, but Margie says his Slurpee is free and wishes him a good day. When we get outside, I tease him. "They like you better than me."

He chuckles. "I helped with a robbery a couple of

months back."

"Someone robbed this 7-Eleven?" Here I thought I lived in a pretty safe part of the city. Then my house gets broken into.

"More often than you think. Best I not tell you."

"Yeah, keep those stats to yourself, thanks. I'd like to have good dreams in the times I actually get sleep."

We lightly chuckle together, and I awkwardly trail my hand over the condensation running down the lid of my Slurpee. "Well, it was good to see you, Detective."

"It's Hunter." He rubs a hand over the back of his neck, showcasing that his tricep workouts have done his body good. "When I'm not on duty."

"Good to see you, Hunter." I try not to blush too hard using his first name. "I'm off to use that porn-filled computer to upload more videos."

"Don't get too distracted by all the earmuffs."

I snort, and I grin the whole way to my car, unable to hide the little jig my flat butt does before I flop into the driver's seat. Oh. My. Gosh. I totally have a thing for the detective handling my case, and I don't give a crappity crap over how taboo that is.

chapter four

Hunter

My fingers slip over the straw in my Slurpee. The condensation has left a ring on my desk, and I consider getting up and grabbing something to clean it, but I can't seem to find the motivation.

A slight smile touches my lips at the image of the straw hitting Hazel on the cheek. I don't think she knew I noticed, but I notice a lot. Part of the job. But even if it wasn't, I think I'd notice a lot about her.

She wore her hair down today. It's short, curly, blonder than I remember. The opening of her loose sweater kept slipping, giving me peeks of her collarbone. She kept rolling the green straw over her teeth, and that damn smile will haunt my dreams for more than just one night.

"Uh… You listening to me?"

I blink, shifting my gaze from the drink to Weir.

"Nope," I tell him with a laugh.

"I figured." His chair squeaks as he leans back. One day that thing will break underneath him, and I'll be ready with my camera. "What's got you so distracted?"

I shake my head. "Just thinking about this case." It's not complete bullshit. But no way in hell am I admitting I'm thinking about the victim in an active case. I'd lose my certification in a second if I pursued Hazel right now. Just more motivation for me to get to the bottom of this burg. As soon as I close it, I'm asking her out.

"I can take it from you, still," he offers a little too eagerly, not meeting my eyes. "I've got room for it."

"I've got it handled."

"It's really not a problem, Stoll." His jaw clenches, and I tilt my head. Weir's a good cop, but he's not a proactive one. He takes what he gets and doesn't complain, but he's not the first to ask for more.

I clear my throat. "If I need help, I'll let you know."

His eyes narrow, but he doesn't push. Cops are good like that. We don't push for more because we all get it. If there's shit, we deal with it in our own way.

He shuts his laptop, unplugging it from its docking station. "Well, I'm heading out. Mal's got an interview this afternoon. I cleared it with Cooke."

"What's she interviewing for?" From what I remember, Weir's wife runs her own business. Maybe she's gotten big enough to hire some employees, and in that case, I need to congratulate her.

He purses his lips, snatching his jacket from the back of his chair. "Business went under. She's determined to find a new job."

My brows rise. "Oh man, I'm sorry. She doing okay?"

"Devastated. She won't let me grab overtime shifts in the meantime. Wants to pull her own weight or some shit. I'm trying to understand it, but damn, I wish she'd just let me do what I can."

"Yeah. There are plenty of OT shifts you could pick up."

"I told her, but she's being stubborn."

"Where is her interview at?"

"Walmart. She said it's better than nothing, but going from running her own shop to this? Don't know how long this will last."

"Can she not build it up again? I know that's a lot of work, but you guys are good financially to do that, right?"

"If she lets me work overtime." He blows out a sigh, looking over his shoulder before continuing. "She's just discouraged. Got some bad PR, and the blowback burnt her out. Any time I even entertain the idea of her picking it back up, she shuts down. It's been rough."

I nod, unsure of how to help other than to listen. "Damn. That sucks."

"It's a shitshow." He pulls his phone from his pocket, checking whatever's on the screen. "I'd commiserate more, but she's wondering if I left yet. I'll see you tomorrow."

"See ya."

He makes quick work of clocking out, and my focus turns to the burg. Hazel mentioned an ex-husband, and I wonder if there's anything there I could investigate. With the primary focus being her gaming stuff, nothing else touched, no forced entry... she very well could be an intentional target.

I pull up YouTube and type in Hazel gaming. She's the top search; her channel named "Hazelnut." The thumbnail of her latest video is a picture of her with a pair of teal headphones over her blonde hair, her eyes wide, her cute mouth frozen in a perfect O. The background is a game I've never seen, but there's a ghostly figure in the doorframe. The title is "My Fans Made Me Pee Myself."

Holding back a laugh, I click the video and slide in my earbuds.

"Hey there, gamers! It's Hazelnut here, and I'm playing a game so many of you told me to since we're in the month of October. Yay Halloween! But you all know I'm a giant baby, so I think that's why you told me to start this one..."

She's adorable. I can't help but let the thought weave through my head. Not only is she attractive, but the way she talks is comfortable, confident, unapologetic. Immediately I worry about her safety. Putting herself out there like this, she's bound to get a slew of messages and comments from creeps.

Keeping her video going, I scroll to read some of them. And yeah, I'm not wrong. There are more good ones than bad, and I'm relieved to see that, but there are the many that bring up how sexy she is, how gorgeous, how they could make her happy. Then there's a few talking about her nipples. Enough that I wonder what the hell it is, because there are so many people laughing in the replies. Almost like the nipple thing is an inside joke, but I sure as hell ain't laughing.

Frustration boils up the back of my neck, and I don't realize how tight my jaw is until my phone rings, and an ache pulses through my teeth as I answer.

"Hello?"

The tired voice of my sister, Sammie, echoes through the receiver. "Hey. You busy?"

"I'm working. Are you okay?"

"I'm fine, Hunt," she says with an exasperated sigh. She's used to my overprotective brothering. "My washer isn't working, and I need these pants for tonight. Thought maybe you could take a look, but I'll call Paxton."

"He'd probably do a better job of fixing it, that's for damn sure." My best buddy is more like an adoptive brother. A very handy one, at that.

She snorts. "Yeah. Why am I calling you again?"

"Because I'm your favorite."

"Sure. Hanging up now."

"Good luck. And behave."

"No." She hangs up, and I set the phone on my desk. Paxton will help her out. He'll either fix the thing or offer his own washer as a substitute. He's good like that. When my parents got divorced, he took the mantle of protective older brother alongside me, and we watched out for Ransom, Miles, Sammie, and Emerson like we'd suddenly become the parents.

My sister relieved a little of the tension in my chest from reading those comments on Hazel's video, and I take a sip of my melted Slurpee and try to put on an objective hat while investigating further. I watch more videos and work my way back, looking for a pattern in the top comments or any particular obsessive ones.

GRLSIMP: You have the most annoying voice. Just die already.

I clench my jaw, doing a search on other videos for the same username. Every video.

GRLSIMP: Why do you even exist?

GRLSIMP: Do yourself a favor and shove that controller up your ass.

GRLSIMP: Gamer girls are so desperate for attention.

Buzz, buzz.

I jolt from my phone, vibrating across my desk. I inhale, cleansing my anger with some oxygen before answering.

"Detective Stoll."

"Um… Hunter?" There's a sniff, and my hackles raise. "I-I mean, Detective."

"Hazel?"

"Y-yeah." She sniffs again, and I'm up and out of my seat.

"Are you safe? Hurt?"

"Someone… My car. Can you… Will you come to my house?"

"On my way." I slam the lid on my laptop down and pull it into my arms. "Lock your door, and don't answer it for anyone."

"O-okay." She lets out a shaky breath as I rush out of the PD building. "Thank you."

chapter five

Hazel

The bright red paint drips down the side of my car, the letters forming words that sting far worse than alcohol in an open wound.

DUMB BITCH

Graphic graffiti surrounds the words, including a crude painting of what is supposed to be me.

I swipe under my eye, hoping to get all the tears out before Hunter gets here, but the tears I swipe away get replaced within seconds.

Why would someone do this to me? To my property? Is this the same person who took my things or a coincidence? All the questions with no answers swirl through my brain, and a dizzy spell hits me. I shut the blinds and sink to the floor, burying my face in my hands.

I've never felt so unsafe in my life. Like someone is out

there, targeting me, stalking me, watching my every move. Watching me right now.

A brush of fur tickles my elbow, and I pull Cheeto into my arms. It's been two minutes since I hung up with Hunter, and I don't know where he is or if he was busy or if I completely made a fool of myself by calling, but my knee is in a constant state of bouncing. I don't think I'll feel safe until he's here, and it'll be agony when he leaves. Would it be awful of me to ask for an officer to station themselves outside my house all night?

The sun sinks farther behind the mountain on the west side, casting my living room in a dark orange glow. I cuddle Cheeto even closer, fear digging its nails into my heart and pumping it faster than it's used to.

A knock comes at the door, and my breath is stolen away. Hunter told me not to answer, and I won't.

"Hazel? It's Hu—Detective Stoll."

I push from the floor, stumbling in my fuzzy socks to get to the door. The moment I open it, relief pries the cold, harsh fingers of fear from my heart, and I resist the urge to crumble into his arms. The sting of fresh tears pricks the backs of my eyes, and I swallow hard.

"You mind if I come in?" he asks, his low voice soft and reassuring. Safe. I nod, stepping aside for him. He brushes by me, his stance tall and proud, strong and brave—everything I need because I can't find any of those things inside me right now.

"Did you see?" I ask through my wet, crackly voice. Those seagreen eyes I like so much flicker with sympathy before they're set in his usual poker face.

"I took some pictures. And I need to ask questions, but I can wait until you're ready."

A tear drops from my chin, and I swipe my cheek. "I don't know anyone who would've done this."

"No idea? You don't have a hateful fan or anything? Your ex and you are on good terms?"

I shake my head. "Kevin wouldn't do this. And I don't think any of my fans even live near here."

"You don't know for sure, though." His eyes remain impassive, but there's sudden tension in his shoulders, a tick in his jaw.

My brow furrows. "Do you think it's one of my viewers?"

The muscles in his forearms flex, and I drop my gaze to his hands on his hips, his fingers clenched. "Maybe," he bites out.

I step forward, enough that the heat from his body radiates across my skin. I beg my voice not to shake when I tell him, "Is… Do you think someone's after me?"

The cop façade falls from his stoic expression, and his hands drop from his hips. He reaches toward me, then seems to think better of it. "I know it's a stupid question, but… are you okay?" His eyes cast toward the driveway for the briefest of seconds, and I know he's avoiding my question with his.

"No." I curl in on myself. "I'm hurt. I'm upset. I'm confused. I'm… I'm scared." I slap my hands over my face, disintegrating like paper in water. I know these feelings all too well, and I'm good at handling them, but without my coping mechanisms—my games, my online world, my distractions—I don't know what to do. I feel… alone.

A low, husky growl erupts from outside my cocoon of despair, and next thing I know, strong, warm arms wrap around me, pulling me tight against a hard, but comforting frame. I sink into Hunter's navy t-shirt, the scent of coffee and leaves mixing in the air. His hand runs up and down my back, and soothing, whispered promises float into my ear.

"I'll find out who did this. I'll keep you safe. It's going to be okay."

His low voice melts my knees and calms the fear running through my nervous system. I want to believe him. I want all those words to be true. And I don't know how he'll keep those promises when I don't think I'll be able to crawl from the comfort of his arms.

"It's not the first time," I say into his shirt before pulling away slightly, but not enough to be out of his hold. I turn my eyes up to meet his. "I've been called stupid my whole life."

His teeth clench, bringing out the faintest dimples underneath his scruff. "Who in the hell thinks that?"

"Lots of people." I snuggle back into his hold, wrapping my arms around his waist and keeping him hostage for as long as he allows. "It's my MO. I'm the airheaded ditz who fails at video games for views. I'm happy-go-lucky, enjoying my life and ignoring the real problems in the world, so I must be stupid. I must be dense. It's amazing I manage to dress myself."

His soothing circles on my back cease, and he takes a deep breath that smells like Slurpee and heaven. "You don't believe that, do you?"

"Most days, no." The words spray-painted on my car flicker through my mind. "Today, yes." I push my face into the comfort of his chest. It's so weird to think that letting him hold me like this feels so safe and calming, but at the same time makes my heart race and my temperature rise.

"You're far from stupid, Hazel."

"You don't really know me. I very well could be."

"That's true, but don't underestimate my detective skills. I've been doing my research."

"Meaning?"

"Watching your videos. Studying the comment section. Putting some theories together."

I shake my head against him. "My videos aren't me. I mean, not really." I try to be authentic, but without meaning to, I put on a show. There's something about being in front of the camera that allows me to be more elaborate, quirkier, dive into my awkwardness and relatability. But when I'm alone… I guess I don't know myself that well either.

"Hazel, I know some pretty stupid people. I deal with them on a daily basis. Sometimes I wrack my brain for excuses to get away from them." His hand slows, resting at the small of my back. "And, well, honestly… I've spent all day coming up with excuses to talk with you again."

The tiniest bit of pressure from his fingertips sends a chorus of butterflies through my stomach. I hope to God this isn't some hero complex playing out, that he isn't holding me because he does this with all the victims of his cases—that somehow I've crawled under his skin the same way he has mine.

I lean away, meeting his gaze. Without much thought in my head, I push up on my toes and press my lips to his.

A grunt of surprise vibrates from the deep recesses of his throat, and I jump away, terror and embarrassment mingling in my cheeks.

"I am… so so sorry…" I sputter, praying he's not studying the redness in my skin. I avoid his eyes, staring at my chonker of a cat. "I often do things before I think about them, and I just…" I throw my hands into the air, because there is no explanation that isn't all-out humiliating.

I like him, he's hot, he's protecting me and that's hella attractive, and he's sweet and smells like a freaking Slurpee.

"It's okay," he says, and his low grumble has my eyes darting to his. His mouth is parted, his gaze dark and focused in on my lips. My heart comes to a standstill, my breath completely gone.

In one second flat, he closes the space between us, taking me into his arms and covering my mouth. The sweet thank you kiss I intended is long gone, morphing into something with more purpose. Excitement bubbles up in me; I want to pinch myself, but I refrain. I slither my hand up his chest, trailing my nails along that sexy as hell jawline. I scratch his light scruff, and he opens his mouth, taking control of the kiss with one smooth tap of his tongue.

His fingers dig into my hips, backing me against the wall. The sound of a picture rocking and crashing to the floor muffles in my ear, my cat hissing and nails scattering across the floor as he darts away. Hunter's hands are everywhere—running over the curve of my ass, pulling at the crook of my knee, gently coaxing my chin, then aggressively pulling at my hair. Every nerve in my body is on fire, and he's gasoline, pouring, pouring, pouring with every touch from his rough palms.

His tongue strokes mine, and he tastes like cherries and Mountain Dew, and I claim that as my new favorite flavor. I claw at him, digging my nails into the tight muscles of his arms, reveling in the fact that he's so strong, so safe, so passionate.

His hot breath cascades over my chin as he moves his kisses downward, across my neck and just under my earlobe. His fingers curl into my right sleeve and tug, uncovering my shoulder. He rakes that fiery tongue of his across my collarbone, dipping it in the hollow and running it to my earlobe where he takes a bite. I die and resurrect in his arms, letting out noises I had no idea I was capable of.

If this is how he kisses, God help me when we get to

the bedroom.

I take his face in my hands, loving the masculine feel of his cheeks and jaw, and bring his lips back to mine. I explore his mouth, meeting his tongue stroke for stroke, forgetting everything in my world except him and this fire he started.

His hand covers my breast and kneads it, melting my kneecaps. I gasp for air, titling my neck as he loves on my skin, moving his grasp down, down, down.

I thank the Lord for lounge pants as his fingers slip easily under the elastic waistband, teasing the hot ache between my legs. Yes, please, I think, and honestly, I'm not sure if I say it out loud. Either way, he obliges, stroking the rough pad of his thumb across me, and I soak his palm in an instant.

"My bedroom," I gasp, wanting him to move me. I want to be comfortable and taken to a place I haven't been since the divorce... and with his touch, maybe a place I haven't been ever. "It's upstairs. To the right. Please don't judge me for the mess."

He freezes. The air in the room changes in an instant. I curse my mouth for talking instead of kissing.

"Or... we can do it here..." I mumble. He backs away like I've thrown a spider on him, the elastic on my pajama bottoms snapping against my waist. He puts his hands in the air, his hair a wild mess from my fingers tugging at the soft strands, a look of horror and embarrassment in those beautiful seagreen eyes.

"I'm sorry," he stutters. "I can't. We can't. I shouldn't have…" He growls at the ceiling, then closes the distance between us once more. His lips meet mine in a soft, sweet kiss that fills my heart in half a second. "I can't do this with you."

"Why?" My bottom lip juts out on its own accord, and he taps it with his index finger.

"Because you're the victim in an active case—one I'm assigned to." He lets out a disappointing, frustrated sigh. "I could lose my badge."

"Really?"

He nods, his hair tickling my forehead. I slump against the wall he's pinned me to.

"Well… shit."

"Yeah."

I cross my arms to keep them from misbehaving. "What about after?"

He lets out a humorless laugh and taps a kiss to the tip of my nose. He steps away, putting about a whole living room of air between us. "My plan was to ask you out as soon as the case was closed."

"Yes," I answer prematurely. "I mean, yes, I want to do that."

"Good." His smile is sad and happy all at once, and I want to eat it up. But I keep my distance like a good girl.

"So… solve the case, then. Chop, chop."

He tosses his head back, his laughter in the top ten

highlights of my day. The list being his tongue, his lips, his scruff, his hands, his chest, his hugs, his scent, his voice, and of course, his eyes.

"I'm on it. But... I need to ask some questions first. If you're ready."

"I think I've been thoroughly comforted."

His ears turn that adorable red as he takes a seat across the room and pulls a pen and pad out. I sit as well, calling Cheeto over so I have something in my lap. I don't want my feet to do their own thing and take me to Hunter.

"Okay, Detective," I say once I snuggle my cat in my arms. "Fire away."

chapter six

Hunter

"Wait, you met a woman? Like a real life one, not something Ransom cooked up in his lab?"

Ransom makes a face at our youngest sister, Emerson, taking the wine away from her.

"Hey!" she grumbles, fighting for it, but she's a shorty who can't compete against Ransom's six-foot-four. "Birthday girl gets all the wine."

"We're teaching you to drink responsibly," Miles says, taking the bottle from Ransom and dodging Hershey, who keeps stepping in his way. "You have to layer. Food first, then more alcohol."

She sticks her tongue out but grabs a roll from the center of the table and chomps a huge bite, chewing obnoxiously.

Sammie takes a roll for herself and turns her attention

to me. "Um, don't get off topic here. Tell us about her."

Five pairs of eyes turn on me, and I turn to every one of my siblings and Paxton before giving in to the pressure.

"Her name's Hazel."

"Hunter and Hazel?" A high-pitched noise escapes Emerson, and Hershey runs over to make sure she's not dying. "That is adorable."

"Don't get too excited," I warn, but I can't help but grin. I grab a beer to hide it. "For all I know, it won't go anywhere."

"Why not?" Paxton asks, taking a seat at the table next to Sammie. She rests her chin on his shoulder, her eyes pinned on me as she chucks a chunk of roll at Hershey, who catches it without any trouble.

"She's a victim in a burg case I'm working on. Can't have anything happen until it's closed."

"So close it," Emerson says around a mouthful of roll. "You said property cases like these are easy peasy."

"I want to recover her things." I take a pull from my beer. "And it's not just the burg. Her car was vandalized, too. She might have upset someone, and they're retaliating."

"Shit, is she okay? Will she have to move or stay somewhere else?" Miles' eyes widen, concern etching his features. He's never been good at hiding his emotions, and his heart is huge, so we get to see that a lot.

"Her house is on a lot of patrol routes. I've asked a few guys to drive by during their night shifts."

"Scary," Sammie says, lifting her chin off Paxton's shoulder. "You have any leads?"

"She's a YouTuber." I shrug. "I've checked a few of her comments. There's one person who keeps leaving her threatening messages. I'm seeing if I can get the IP address traced."

"Isn't Weir good at that?" Miles asks, sliding into a seat and grabbing a roll for himself. He tosses his head, trying and failing to get his long, unruly hair to stay out of his face.

"Yeah. He's dealing with some personal shit, though. Haven't had a chance to ask him."

"I can do it," Sammie volunteers, her loose bun of blonde hair bouncing with her excitement. "If it's not, like, against the law or anything."

I chuckle. "Yeah, that'd be great. Thanks."

"Yep." She picks up her phone. "What's her channel name?"

"Hazelnut Gaming."

"Cute." She taps away on her screen, and Emerson nods toward the wine sitting by Ransom. He grudgingly slides it over, and she pours herself a very full glass.

"Happy twenty-first birthday to me," she says, and they all laugh… except me.

"You aren't driving tonight, right?"

"No, Dad," she teases, then takes a long sip.

Ransom sets his drink down, furrowing his brow. "Gotta say, Hunt, I'm a little confused."

"About…?"

"Don't know. Just didn't picture you as a guy who'd go for a gamer."

"You jealous?" Paxton teases Ransom. "She's nerdy and geeky and that's your thing, right?"

"Hell yeah. Just didn't know it ran in the family." He tips his beer at me. "So… what do you like about her?"

"Um, she's hot as hell," Sammie pipes up for me, her mouth dropped open as she stares at her phone.

"Ooh, let me see." Emerson wiggles her fingers, asking for the phone. She spins the screen around, playing the video. Hazel's cute voice fills the room, and her jokes land with every one of my siblings.

"Hunt, can I make a move on her?" Emerson asks, sitting back in her seat and flipping her wavy brown hair over her shoulder. "Just keep her warm for you until you solve this case?"

"You keep your hands to yourself," I warn, only half joking. My baby sister is far more appealing than she thinks she is, and I don't want to risk losing Hazel to her. Not that I have Hazel in any way. "And yes, she's very cute."

"Cute? You're using the word cute?" Sammie asks.

"Is there something wrong with cute?"

"It's so… meaningful."

Ransom, Miles, Paxton, and I all share equally confused glances, but the girls seem to understand what the hell that means.

"Look, I like being around her. Talking to her. She

amuses me. Makes me laugh."

"You? Laughing?" Emerson's eyes widen, and she shakes her head at the table. "I have to meet this girl."

"I hope you solve this case for her soon," Miles says, always the voice of concern. "Get her stuff back. She can't stream, right?"

"Not really. Her latest upload explains all that."

"And Superman here gave her his laptop, from the sounds of it." Sammie nods to her phone screen, plopping a maraschino cherry into her mouth.

"Wait… can't you get in trouble for that?" Paxton asks as he wipes crumbs off his grease-stained denim overshirt. He just got off work before he made his way over.

I lift a shoulder. "Not sure, to be honest." But I really hope the department doesn't find out. I hope they don't find out about a lot of things I've done with Hazel.

The reminder of her body, the feel of her skin against my palms, her lips and tongue and taste… all of it shoots through my mind, and I shake my head to rid myself of it. I can't think about that now, of how much shit I'd be in.

How I'm pretty sure it was worth it.

"Um, Hunt," Sammie says, pulling me from my head. "This GRLSIMP person… that's who you're talking about, right?"

"Yeah."

She turns her phone around, showing me a profile page. "They live in Hazel's city."

chapter seven

Hazel

I stretch, pushing my arms to the sky and letting out a deep exhale. That was the best nap I've ever had, and I owe it all to Hunter. He'll never know it, of course. But after that unbelievable kiss a few days ago, I've fantasized about that during my alone time.

I check the clock on my nightstand. 4:32. Awesome. I'll order some dinner and get to commenting. With streaming off the table for a bit, I've decided to take this time and respond to some comments. I rarely get the chance anymore, only giving comments some hearts between editing my videos. A buzz of excitement tickles my ribcage as I bounce my way to the living room, parking my butt in my comfy chair and pulling Hunter's laptop out.

"Okay," I tell myself, "it's definitely a pasta night." I swear I'm Doordash's number one customer as I click the app and pick my usual at Noodles n' Company. It gives the old laptop enough time to boot up, so when I put my phone down on the arm of the chair, my YouTube profile is ready for me.

My last video has 1.2M views, and I bite away a gleeful grin. Anything over 10K is a win. Over a mil is worth ten thousand Coke Slurpees. My happy heart pumps as I peruse through the top comments. Thank heavens my viewers are mostly supportive and understanding, genuine people. There are the few who are butts just to be butts, but some of my viewers jump in and call them trolls or tell me to ignore them or defend me. It took a couple of years for me to grow my thick skin, but I'm a Mountain Man now with the hide I've developed.

I take a deep breath. "Okay, let's dive in."

Back in the day, I was able to respond to every comment made, and as I type away, my smile growing, I realize how much I miss that. Maybe I need to carve out a day for responding. It's good for the soul to interact like this.

About a half hour into work, my doorbell rings, and I squeal and rush for my food. But when I swing my door open, there's no yummy cheese tortellini waiting for me, but a thick, white envelope. My brows pinch, and I pick it up, taking it inside.

There's no name on it. Not sure if it's truly meant for me or if it's one of those packets of coupons or something. I slip my finger under the flap and tear it open. A peek of a photo piques my curiosity, and I pull it out.

My stomach hollows, and my throat dries in an instant. It's a photo of me and Hunter outside 7-Eleven. I'm nursing my Slurpee while he holds his at his side. The picture looks like it was taken near one of the gas pumps.

I flip it around, looking for a caption or message, but there isn't one. I dig through the rest of the pictures. One of me outside grabbing my mail. One of me looking out my front window at my spray-painted car. Another of Hunter taking pictures of the car. Me at the library, Hunter leaving my house after kissing me, a shot of me washing my car.

Then there are some I know this person didn't take. Photos that were on my computer. Thumbnails of my videos, selfies uploaded from my phone, and private photos I sent Kevin when we were married.

The photos shake in my hands, terror burning the backs of my eyes and pouring down my cheeks. I rush to my door, slapping the deadbolt in place. I shut the blinds, Cheeto growling from the lack of a sunbeam on the rug. Panic surges through my muscles, and I race through my house, shutting every window, closing every curtain, locking every door. I curl into a ball in my kitchen, hiding in the corner where my sink meets the bar. My hands curl around my phone, my fingers shaking as I scroll for Hunter's number.

"Detective Stoll."

"I just got an envelope full of pictures," I rush out,

hoping my voice isn't plagued with just how freaked out I am. "It was dropped off at my door."

"Pictures of what?" he asks, his voice firm, unafraid, all-business, no-nonsense, and exactly what I need.

"Me. You. At my house, at the gas station. Through my window. And some from my computer."

"You still have them?"

"Yes."

"Good. I'm on my way. I'll run them for prints. Stay inside and lock the doors."

"Already done."

The longest twenty minutes pass by, and my phone rings. I answer it, my muscles aching as I stand from my huddled position on the floor.

"You here?" I ask without saying hello.

"At your door."

Relief floods through me, and I run to let Hunter in. He's holding my food in one hand, his phone in the other. "Did you see a car parked out front?" he asks.

I shake my head. "I thought it was my food. I wasn't really paying attention…"

He sets the bag on my side table, shutting the door behind him. Without a seconds' hesitation, he pulls me into his warm and safe arms.

"Do you have somewhere to stay?"

The scent of leaves I'm starting to associate with him fills the air. "No."

"No friends? Family?"

"Kevin, maybe. But that'd be a little awkward."

"Not him." His body tenses underneath my cheek, and I don't know if it's suspicion or jealousy that has him worked up, but I don't ask. Kevin wouldn't do this. I know it in my bones.

"There's no one else. My family doesn't live in the state, and all my friends are… Well, they're virtual."

He runs his hands up and down my back before pulling away to look me in the eye. "I'm staying here."

I hold back from crying in relief. "What about your job? You can't… I won't let you risk losing your badge."

"I'm going to stay in my car." He pushes a lock of hair behind my ear, leaving fire in his wake that burns my forehead and caresses my heart. "Watch your house and keep an eye out."

"All night?"

"I'm used to night shifts." The smallest of grins teases the corner of his mouth, and I know he's only doing that to reassure me, and he's just as worried as I am over this thing. But I appreciate it. Just his presence is reassuring.

"Can I at least share dinner with you?"

He tilts his head back and forth. "Yeah, I think that'll be fine."

I swallow hard, still too scared to smile, even though I'm thrilled he's here, and he'll be here all night. "Okay, good." I take the bag, and before I lead him into the kitchen, I jump into his arms again for a quick hug. There isn't much we can do, and I'm not willing to risk his job, but I'm so grateful to him at this moment. I need to tell him in some way just how much.

chapter eight

Hunter

I scan the road after a flash of movement catches my eye. A small cat skitters across the front yard on the corner before disappearing into the bushes. My heart relaxes, even though my nerves are on high alert.

It's been quiet outside Hazel's place—only the buzz of the streetlamp and the occasional radio call keeping me company. I tap the steering wheel with one hand while rubbing the scruff along my chin with the other. I can't remember the last time I did a stake out. The cases I've been assigned lately haven't called for it, and when they do, Weir is usually in the seat next to me.

Another flash of movement has my gaze rushing to the yellow front door. Hazel steps onto her porch, the moon reflecting off the silver spot in the design of her hoodie. Looks like lettering—I can't make it out from here, not with the tray of mugs she's carrying.

I climb from the front seat, stepping onto the road, the crunch of loose asphalt filling the air. She offers a shy grin, holding the tray out for me.

"I didn't know if you were a coffee drinker, but I brought you some caffeine options."

My lips press into a thin line. "You should be inside."

She lifts a shoulder. "I can't sleep." She jostles the tray slightly, a few of the mugs tipping their contents. "You sure I can't tempt you?"

The bags under my eyes must be giving me away. Night shifts haven't been on my schedule for a while, and my body isn't used to it.

"What are my choices?" I lean to check all the different mugs. I have a few solid guesses—straight black coffee in the Mickey Mouse mug, cream and sugar in the Santa mug. But there's one that's clear and bubbly, leaving me completely clueless.

"Well, we have your straight up black coffee," she starts, nodding to Mickey Mouse. "Then some cream and sugar."

I know my coffees, I'm proud to say.

"Then there's just milk, just sugar," she continues, nodding to the respective mugs, which include an orange tabby cat head and a Darth Vader goblet. "And if you aren't a coffee man, there's hot chocolate spiked with Coke. I know you're thinking gross, but trust me on this one." Her hazel eyes light up at the whipped cream confection dribbling down the sides of a blue phone booth that I think has something to do with Doctor Who, but I'm not a hundred percent sure of that.

"And what's this?" I point to the clear bubbles in a wide mug shaped like a cupcake.

"Red bull." She lifts a shoulder. "The tray looked weird with just the can on it."

A laugh trickles from my gut, and I grab Mickey Mouse. Her shoulders slump forward, and she lets out a long sigh.

"Thank you for not taking longer to decide. My arms are killing me."

I quickly put the mug back and take the tray from her. "Thank you." I tell her. "You didn't have to."

"I did it for me, really." She rubs her upper arms, and I catch some of the writing on her hoodie. Gamer is the first word, glinting in silver letters. Her arms cover the word below it. "I'm going nuts in there alone."

I nod toward the porch. "You want to keep me company for a bit?"

"Yes, please."

We take a spot on the top step, and I set the tray of mugs behind us. She picks up the hot chocolate.

"Glad you didn't take this one. I was hoping for it." She snuggles up to the mug, taking a sip and leaving a dollop of whipped cream on her nose.

"Hot chocolate tends to put me to sleep," I say, boldly

swiping the cream for her. "I get the sugar crash."

"Hence the Coke spiking."

"Coke has sugar in it."

"Yes, it does," she says proudly, her eyes bulging as she takes another giant sip. Her excitement is infectious, and I wish I could bottle that up and take it with me.

"So… I'm impressed with your mug collection," I say after taking my own sip, gazing Mickey in the overalls.

"It's part of my thing." She waves a nonchalant hand. "The whole gamer, streamer, YouTube persona. I have a fun mug sitting on my desk, and people like to comment on it. I get sent a lot as well, and I give shoutouts to people who gift them to me. This one's my favorite." She points to the cat.

"That's the creepiest one."

She drops her mouth open in mock shock. "It's adorable!"

"The eyes aren't the same size."

"No one's eyes are perfectly symmetrical."

I shake my head, letting her win the argument. "So, if you weren't a streamer, what kind of mugs would you own?"

"Probably none," she says with a laugh.

"Not much for coffee?"

"Oh, I love my coffee…" Her eyes get big again. "Which is super funny because I thought everyone was a coffee drinker. I grew up with it always around. Every friend's house smelled like coffee before school; a coffee maker was like a staple in every kitchen. Then I move here, and I got the shock of my life learning that it's not everyone's thing. A lot of people don't even own coffee makers." She nods toward my mug. "I wasn't sure if you even drank it."

"So you weren't just trying to show off your mug collection?" I tease.

"Well, maybe a little. I don't have many people I can share them with. Not in real life, anyway."

There's a hint of sadness in her tone that doesn't match her expression. "You don't have many friends around?"

She shakes her head. "My family is in Kansas. I moved out here to be with Kevin."

"Your ex-husband?"

"Yep."

My grip tightens on the handle of the mug, the glove of Mickey biting into my knuckle. "Um… do you mind if I…?"

"Ask about my divorce?" she finishes for me with a humorless laugh. "It isn't all that exciting."

"I'm more curious about how you met each other, how long you were married, why you stayed here instead of moving back ho—" I clamp my lips shut, willing my curiosity to shut the hell up since none of it is my business. I'm not allowed to ask her out, let alone pry into her private world just for my own shits and giggles.

Or to make myself feel better about her previous relationships.

"Sorry," I mumble, covering my word vomit with a sip of black.

"For what?" Her cute brows pull together, and she turns to face me, her knees bumping into my thigh. A shot stronger than caffeine runs up my leg. "I don't mind talking about it. Chatting keeps me warm."

She snorts at her own joke, and I wish all to hell I could take my coat off and drape it over her shoulders. But the policy says my uniform stays on me. I've made exceptions before, like when I had to pull a four-year-old out of a frozen pool. I wrapped him in this very coat and held him until the paramedics arrived. Since then, I've carried a blanket and a stuffed animal in the trunk of my car. Just in case.

My eyes dart to the skin peeking from the neck of her hoodie, studying the goosebumps peppered across her milky skin, and I internally swear and shrug my coat off. I put it over her shoulders without thinking more of it.

She snuggles into its warmth, red blossoming on her cheeks. "I didn't mean for you to give up your coat, but thanks." Her nose presses into the neck, and she takes a deep inhale.

"It probably doesn't smell that great," I tease.

"On the contrary. It smells like you."

"And how do I smell?"

"Like leaves." Her eyes widen slightly. "Um… not that

I've noticed or anything."

My spine relaxes, and my mind catches up to just how stiffly I was sitting. Guess I'm more tense than I realized. I should be used to the high alert setting, but it still manages to surprise me.

"To answer your earlier questions," she says, sweeping her stray hair from her ponytail back. She ticks them off on her fingers as she speaks. "I met Kevin online. He's a gamer. I'm a gamer. It was a match made in Minecraft. We were married for one year, three months. And I moved to Utah because I fell in love, and funnily enough, that's why I stayed."

I furrow my brow and set my drink on the tray. "Someone else?"

"No." She lets out a dreamy sigh and leans to look around me. She thrusts her hand out. "How can someone not fall in love with those?"

I follow her gaze, the moon shining off the mountainside, reflecting the snow. I turn back to her. "You're a fan of the mountains."

"They're gorgeous. And they are everywhere."

I chuckle, giving her a nod. "Can't say I disagree, but seeing as I've never known a place without them, maybe I take them for granted."

"You've never gone outside of the state?"

"Nope. I'm a homebody."

"Anywhere you'd like to visit?"

I shake my head. "Truth be told, I don't think about it much." It's not like I have anyone to travel with or the money to do so or the time or the desire. "Maybe Disneyland."

"A-freaking-men. I could go right now. Maybe I'll see how far my stalker follows."

It comes out light, but as her joke floats between us, the air grows thick, and I scan the street again for any sign of unusual activity. There are no cars, no cats… nothing but the two of us, whisper-chatting in the cold, October air.

She has my uniform jacket, and I'm sitting much too close, and if there is someone watching, getting pictures, I can say goodbye to this case, if not my entire career.

She sets her hand between us on the porch, her pinky slightly grazing mine. I swallow hard, wishing I could take that hand, entwine my fingers with hers, but I pull away, sliding so there is at least a foot between our bodies.

A frown sets on her lips, and she shakes her head. As if this is her fault. "Sorry."

My voice sort of shorts out, and I garble out something between "It's okay" and "don't worry about it," and she wrinkles her nose and laughs at my nonsense response.

"You know," she says, "one of these days we'll actually get to touch each other, and it'll be glorious."

"You think, huh?"

"I know so." She takes a sip, then puts her mug on her knees. "But then you'll have your way with me and that'll be it." She lets out a dramatic, playful sigh, letting me know she doesn't believe that, but it stings anyway. My defenses rise, and I shift forward, leaning toward her.

"I told my siblings about you."

Her playful smile warps into something a little more curious. "About the case…?"

"A little about that," I admit. "But mostly about how much I like you." I scratch at my scruff, scanning the street again before meeting her eyes. "And just so you know, telling my siblings is… sort of a big deal. Not to freak you out or anything."

She licks her lips, wiping a spot of whipped cream that got caught in the corner. I drop my hand, tangling my fingers together to keep myself from rubbing my beard off.

"I just don't want you to think I'm a person who… how did you say it? Has his way with you?"

She lets out a shaky laugh… soft and free and adorable, and my heart runs at the same beat. "It's a big deal?"

"Telling my siblings? Oh yeah." The merciless teasing I'll receive over the next few months is a rite of passage. And I imagine the abuse I'll be subjected to will last much longer, considering I don't date much. Or at all.

"How many do you have again?"

"Two brothers, two sisters." I pause. "But then there's Paxton and Oakley and Joy and Evan…"

"Did you adopt another family?" She snorts.

"Nah, but we all have friends who are like family. When my parents split, my best friend kinda helped me and my siblings get through it. He became a brother to me. Oakley and Joy and Evan did the same for Sammie and Ransom and Miles."

"Oh, I can't wait for you to introduce me to all these people, and I will instantly forget all their names."

I laugh a little louder than I mean to, and the cat down the street runs across a couple of lawns. "I can't wait for that either."

Her eyes drop to my hand, and her grip tightens on her mug. "You're lucky, you know? To have so many people."

"You have millions of them, from what I see."

"Subscribers, yes. And I don't feel lonely or anything, and I know I'm super lucky in a lot of ways, but… I don't know, being online sometimes makes me feel like people only enjoy that version of me."

"You seem pretty damn authentic in your videos."

"I try to be. But still… it happens. The fake smile, the reassurance that all is well. Or even the pressure to not complain, because what do I have to complain about? I'm young, pretty, and have money. Boo hoo."

"Sounds like you're reading too many hate-filled comments."

She tilts her head. "So you've read them, too?"

My jaw clenches. "I was digging. Looking for motive." There's a fan around the corner from here I'm going to pay a little visit to in the morning, but I don't want to worry Hazel unnecessarily.

"I promise my skin is thick." She eyes her hot

chocolate, the whipped cream melting into the liquid. She plays with the spoon tucked inside the mug and stirs the cream until it disappears. "I just… I guess I wonder if I know who I am at all. If I've spent so much of my life in front of a screen that it's now who I've become. My whole identity. And that's a lot to stomach for some people. Most people, actually. If I'm on your screen, and you get tired of me, then you can click away, no biggie. In real life… Well, it's a lot more awkward to just walk away from a conversation."

If only she knew how hard it was to walk away from her. My lips pull down at the corners. "I think you are being hard on yourself."

"Maybe." Her nail taps against her mug, and the clink echoes in the small space between us. "I guess I'm unfamiliar with face-to-face interactions. Kevin and I got so used to gaming and streaming all the time that we realized we only liked each other when there was a screen between us. I worry other people will feel that way about me."

"Perhaps this robbery is a blessing in disguise," I say with a smirk. "Teach you to get out a little more."

"You shut your dirty mouth." She nudges me with her foot, and if I weren't on duty, if I wasn't the detective on her case, I'd grab her ankle, slide her toward me, and meet her smiling lips with my own.

Instead, I keep my ass planted, and we talk well into the night, until the sun starts its ascent over those mountains I'm so happy she fell in love with.

chapter nine

Hunter

I lift my hand and give the dark blue door a knock, then step off the porch.

I'm beat. I don't know how I'm still standing. But I blink and rub my eyes, hoping to hell they aren't bloodshot red from my all-nighter.

"Hello?" a woman, mid-forties I'd say, asks, her door open just a peek. Her hair is up in a towel, her face fresh from a shower. It's early, I realize, and I instantly apologize.

"Sorry for the hour, ma'am. I'm Detective Stoll. I'm investigating a burglary that happened a couple of streets over. Would you mind if I ask you some questions?"

Her eyes widen, and she opens the door fully. "A burglary? Oh, that's awful. Yes, I'll help." She stands back to let me inside, but I shake my head, remaining on the bottom step of her porch. Without backup, I prefer the safety of the public eye.

I pull my notepad out and click my pen open, then start my questioning. She doesn't look the type to bully someone online, but my hackles are up, and I watch every expression, every small movement as she answers. Her left leg keeps bouncing, and when I ask her about any unusual people in the neighborhood, her eyes shift to over my right shoulder.

"Ma'am?" I prod when she doesn't answer right away.

"Um…" She blinks and turns toward me. "I've seen a car pass by a few times. I thought maybe it was just family visiting or friends. I can't say I know everyone, but…"

Her voice cuts off, and I put my notepad down. "Do you remember the make or model? Color?"

"Silver. Smaller… I think a four-door, maybe. I'm not familiar with cars."

"Okay. And it drove by a few times?"

She nods. "And I see it parked by the stop sign. It's been there every day for the past few weeks."

"Have you seen the driver?"

Her lips turn down. "No, sorry."

I take a deep breath, forcing a smile. "That's okay. You've been helpf—"

"Mom?" a deep voice from inside calls, and if he hadn't just said "mom" I would've thought he was this woman's brother or husband from the baritone.

He steps onto the porch, and I instantly recognize the protective air around him as he reaches for his mother. Six-three, no doubt—I'm the same height. Long, dark, scraggly hair and a t-shirt that sports a masked man I know from Mortal Kombat. He's wearing basketball shorts, which makes my mind go to teenager. High school, most likely; the acne on his chin isn't as prominent as middle schoolers, but still noticeable.

"This is a detective, Marcus. He's investigating a burglary that happened around here."

Marcus purses his lips, narrowing his eyes. "Hazel, right?"

My brows rise. "You know her?"

He shakes his head. "Not personally. I follow her streams."

"Oh, is she one of those YouTubers you like?" His mom says, adjusting the towel on her head. "What a small world."

What a small world, indeed. I clear my throat, taking my notepad out again. "Ma'am, do you mind if I ask your son some questions? Maybe he's noticed something."

"I haven't." He steps back, taking his mom with him. "And I have to get ready for school."

I watch them both, not wanting to scare them off from telling me more, so I reach into my pocket and pull my card out. "All right, well, thank you for your time. If you see or hear anything, please give me a call. We want to keep the neighborhood safe."

"Of course." She takes it from me, stretching her arm as far as it will go, since Marcus is all but dragging her inside.

"Thank you, Detective."

As the door clicks shut, echoing down the early morning street, my mind swirls. If I had Weir next to me, I know he'd confirm my suspicions. If this GRLSIMP lives in this house, I'd bet all my money it's Marcus. If he does have something to do with the burg and the vandalism and the pictures, he's in a prime location for it. And he might not be working alone; there's a silver car I'm going to keep my eyes peeled for.

My phone buzzes as I slump into the front seat, the car door not even closed as I read the message from Weir.

Get here asap. IA wants to meet with you.

Internal affairs. Well, shit.

chapter ten

Hazel

A wisp of fur tickles my nose, and I swat at it, my brain trying and failing to get out of the in-between sleep.

"Cheeto, stooop," I whine at my cat, who continues to wave his tail across my upper lip. I growl and roll over, snuggling deeper into the covers, fighting the thoughts that want to push me from sleep to awake.

Hunter stayed till seven in the morning when he said he needed to go check a few things before heading into the office. Nothing significant happened while he watched the house, unless I count the slight touch of his pinky against mine, the amusement in his seagreen eyes over my mug collection, or the fact he admitted he liked me. I figured he did, what with the kissing, but a girl likes to hear it out loud.

The moment he left, I worried fear would take hold of me, and I'd be jumping at every sound. Thankfully, sleep overrode fear, and I zonked out.

I wonder what time it is now. Did I get a full eight hours? If I did, that'd be a first in a long time. I'm used to playing games well into the night and sleeping for four to five hours before "clocking in" again.

I grumble into my pillow. Great, my brain is up, so I might as well make an effort to get my body up, too. I reach for my phone, much to the chagrin of Cheeto who growls as I push his butt.

4:43. Wow. More than eight hours. Good for me.

I scroll through a few notifications until I get to a group of people wondering where I am. My brow furrows, and then it hits me. I had a live stream scheduled for four.

I sit straight up, try to fix my hair, and go live.

"Hey wonderful humans. Sorry… I took a much-needed nap and overslept. I'm here now to answer questions. No gaming today… again." I blow a raspberry. "My computer is still missing, but… but… hang in there with me! I might not be playing the game, but I have many thoughts on it. So let's have a conversation…"

My viewers are up to nearly 1k, and I thank the app for alerting so many of them that I'm live. I sit back against my headboard, answering their questions on the new update for a game I've played on my channel for a while. I got the early release—creator privilege—and I'm partway through answering a question about the new journal system when a knock comes at my door.

My heart clutches up, then fast forwards. "Oh, there's

someone at my door. To be continued!"

I throw a hoodie on over my tank top and shove my phone into the pocket. My viewers are used to this kind of break, so I don't worry too much about giving them the view of the inside of my pocket.

The curtains are still drawn, leaving my normally bright living room in darkness. I take a deep breath and push the curtain to the side, spotting an unfamiliar car parked against my curb.

The knock comes again. "Miss Bardot? It's the police."

Police? Hunter is the detective on my case. Would anyone else be here? Is that normal?

"Um… sorry," I say through the door. "But I don't want to open the door to someone I don't know."

A muffled laugh filters through. "Good. I'm glad you're taking precautions. I'm going to slip my card through the door. I'm Detective Weir. I'm Detective Stoll's partner."

Hunter has a partner? I feel like if he was partnered, then I'd have met this detective before now.

The name is familiar. Weir. I've heard it before. Maybe Hunter told me.

A small piece of paper slips through the door by the deadbolt. I take it, looking it over. My heart pounds, and I'm tempted to text Hunter and find out where he is and why this other guy is here.

"I only want to get caught up on this case from your perspective," he says through the door. "I've been asked to take over."

My gaze shoots up from the card to my door, and curiosity grabs hold of me. I flip the deadbolt and open the door a crack.

He's in a uniform; that's promising. It's the same patch on the shoulder, actual equipment on his belt, a badge on his chest. He offers a reassuring grin.

"Where's Hu—Detective Stoll?"

His grin turns sad. "If you give me two minutes, I'll explain everything. Can I come in?"

I debate it in my head for much longer than I should, but he's patient with me. He does look like a cop, and his car must be an unmarked, just like Hunter's. My teeth pull at my bottom lip, and then I step back and let him in.

"Thank you." He slides past me, standing just inside my entryway.

"Um, can I get you a drink or something?" I ask, my voice quavering. Worry for myself and for Hunter mingle together, making a confusing cocktail I've overdosed on.

"I'm fine, thank you." His eyes move to the furniture, and I shake my head, waving an arm for him to take a seat.

"So, where's Detective Stoll?" I ask again as soon as he's settled in my reading chair. He swipes his hand over the arm, sending a wave of orange fur into the air.

"He's been asked to step away from this case. I don't know if this is a surprise to you, but he's grown too attached, so Internal Affairs had to step in."

"Is he in trouble?" Oh gosh, if he loses his job because

of me…

"They're investigating it." He adjusts on the seat, resting his elbows on his knees. A wedding ring catches the light and draws my attention. "I've read the report, but I'd like to hear it from your mouth. You had a few things taken?"

I nod slowly, my brain on Hunter. He's under investigation? Would they find out about the kiss? Is that a fireable offense?

I should've kept my damn lips to myself.

"Hazel?"

I blink, trying to focus on the question. "Um… yeah. They took my computer. All my gaming stuff."

His lips turn down at the corners. He's not taking notes. "Hunter told me you were a gamer of some sort. That must be tough for you."

"It makes it hard to game without a computer," I say with a hollow laugh.

"There was also some vandalism? Pictures?"

"Yeah. My car." I catch him up with that. He still doesn't write anything, and while Hunter's face was usually impassive, completely professional, this guy… Well, it seems like the more I tell him, the more anxious he gets. His butt keeps sliding closer and closer to the edge of his seat, his eyes widening and locked on me, almost like he's studying my every expression.

"Did he have any leads?" I ask, shifting on the couch

cushion. "He was supposed to run the pictures for prints."

"A few."

That's all I get, and a chill goes across the back of my neck. I'm probably paranoid—scared of anyone.

"That's really all of it," I say, rising to my feet. "Thanks for comin—"

"You know, my wife's a big fan of yours." He remains seated, but something is pricking my nerves, and my body refuses to relax.

"Oh, that's nice." My voice isn't stable, and I don't know why. I'm confused and anxious, and I want to call Hunter just to check in with him. But I'm also terrified that calling him would get him in more trouble.

Weir nods, spinning his wedding ring around his finger. "She would watch your streams during her downtime at the shop. She ran a little café, you see."

I swallow hard and force a smile. I'm just paranoid. He's telling me a sweet story about his wife. He only wants an autograph or something, I'm sure.

I force my butt back onto the couch. "Is her café around here?"

"Used to be. She closed up a few weeks ago."

"I'm sorry to hear that."

He stops playing with his ring, his eyes flicking to meet mine. My heart stutters at the glossy wall. "Been rough on her. That shop was everything. Built it from the ground up." He shifts, and I tense, but he only reaches into his pocket, grabbing his phone. He starts scrolling. "August third. Do you remember that day?"

"Can't say I do," I admit with a wobbly laugh.

"You streamed for a good hour and a half. Short one, according to Mal."

I assume Mal is his wife. "I'm usually on for four or five, yes."

"Well, you had a couple of things to say during that stream. She was so excited."

I wrack my brain, wishing I could remember dates and things I had scheduled, but I'm not the most organized person, and most of my streams I ramble on and on about things I don't even know—

"...ready for this crazy story? I found this little place outside Salt Lake..."

My voice echoes from the speaker on his phone, the sounds of a shooter game going on in the background. It's one of my story streams, when I talk about funny things that happen to me while I game. It's one of my more popular segments.

"You came into her shop a few days before this," he says, anger replacing the glossy wall he'd built in his eyes. My fingers curl into the sleeves of my hoodie, every hair on the back of my neck on its end. "She was so thrilled to see you. So happy to have you, of all people, visit her little café. She gave you complimentary coffee and cakes." He tilts his head. "But you're used to that, aren't you? Free stuff."

I remain silent, my brain trying and trying to find a way

to get him out of my house. I know the rest of the story. I remember it now, and I thought I was just being funny, quirky, cute. I exaggerated a lot of it, and I made sure not to make fun of the gal who helped me there. The place just wasn't my cup of tea. It was dirty and there was a long hair baked into the cake. When I got up to leave, my phone stuck to the tabletop. The store was advertised as a coffee and reading place. It was a cute concept with poor execution… which I said in multiple different ways during that stream.

Regret and guilt wash through me, and it amplifies my fear. I couldn't have single-handedly destroyed his wife's business. Could I have?

I rise to my feet, and he follows. He stands much taller than I do, and with all his gear, he's a thousand times more intimidating. But I force my voice to be unwavering. "I think you are the one too attached to this case, Detective. Please leave."

He laughs, and it crawls up my spine and puts acid on the back of my tongue.

"No. I don't think I will."

chapter eleven

Hunter

My heart wouldn't stop its erratic beating when I stepped into IA, but turned out, they were confused as hell. Guess Weir was misinformed or something; Internal Affairs didn't want to meet with me at all.

I'm still on a relief high when I get into my car after my shift. I was fully prepared to admit everything with Hazel and get put on admin leave. Honesty is always best when it comes to that sort of thing. My best hope was to be off for a couple of weeks before going back to work. I'm grateful I don't have to worry at the moment, but the scare has lit a fire under my ass. I'm going to solve this case or pass it over. More alone time with Hazel is too risky.

I'm turning into her neighborhood to check for a silver car when my phone buzzes with a number I don't recognize.

"Detective Stoll," I answer via Bluetooth.

A throat clears. "Uh… is this the detective who came to my house earlier?"

Surprise grips me, recognition sparking at the deep voice. "Marcus?"

"Yeah. I, uh, I think Hazel's in trouble."

My brow furrows, and I turn the wheel to head to his place. Maybe he has more information he wasn't telling me. "All right. What's going on?"

"She went live, and while she was streaming, someone came to her door. It's… Well, it's a little muffled, but he sounds kinda threatening."

I step on the gas, rushing right past his house toward Hazel's. "What can you hear?"

"Some guy. She's asking him to leave, and he won't."

"Can you see anything? Does she have her camera positioned somewhere?"

"It's in her pocket. Picture is black. But from the chat, they're all kinda freaking out. The guy is telling her she destroyed his wife's business or something. Sounds like he has a gun. I told them I'd call you."

"Good." My heart is in my throat, lead in my feet… and there's a silver car in Hazel's driveway. One I recognize in an instant. "I'm here. Thank you, Marcus."

"Should I stay on the phone?"

"Keep watching the stream. I'll figure out what's going on."

He thanks me and hangs up, and I push from the front

seat. Weir's here—I know the car from anywhere. Pieces of our conversations click into place in my brain, and I don't want to believe it, but it makes sense the longer I think. The anger in his eyes whenever I brought up the case, the eagerness to help out or take over, the IA call this morning, and the silver car.

Mal's shop going under. He sunk to this for his wife.

A month ago, I wouldn't have understood in the slightest. Now…?

I call Cooke, tell him to get patrol out here asap. Hazel's in there—alive for the moment, and I'll need backup. I don't trust myself to remain calm, talk him down… not when she's in there.

I get to the front door, approaching quietly, praying he hasn't looked out the front window. My stomach sinks as I draw my weapon, hating I have to use it for protection against someone I've known for half my career.

My gut tells me not to knock, and I listen to it, pushing the door open. A small yipe falls from Hazel's lips, and Weir takes a step from her, the menace in his eyes instantly replaced with a mask I know all too well.

"Stoll," he says with a laugh, the friendly demeanor I've known coming out. Anger and betrayal ripple up my spine. "Thought you were off this case."

My eyes flick to Hazel, terror written in every clenched muscle. Her arms are straight at her sides, her shoulders up by her ears. Her jaw is tight and her eyes wide, almost as if she's frozen and unable to scream.

"Weir," I manage around my own clenched jaw, begging my body to go to autopilot. Get into training mode. I need to de-escalate. I need to be unattached. I need to lie through my teeth.

But he knows all the tricks, and Hazel is in danger, and my mind and my gut say different things.

His gaze drops to my hand, his smile fading. He gets his gun up and pointed at Hazel before I can even raise mine.

"Drop it."

I don't. "You really want to do this?" I ask him, begging my voice to stay even. "You're going to lose your badge."

"I'm going to lose it anyway," he spits, jutting his gun at Hazel, who winces at the movement. My heart thumps against my chest, echoing in my ears. Weir is the top marksman in our department. He won't miss, no matter how far Hazel stands from him.

I shake my head, scrambling. "It's just the three of us. No one knows about anything. Just me."

"You haven't skipped off to Cooke?" He snorts. "Thought you'd do that the moment you put it together. Figured you were here to claim your prized pussy."

A shaky breath escapes me, and I tamp the anger down. "Cooke doesn't know shit." I nod toward Hazel's gaming room. "I'll help you cover it up. Hazel can promise to let the case close unsolved. You keep your badge, she has to buy her way back into business, we all win."

He presses his lips together. "That's not what I want."

"What, then?"

His eyes flash to Hazel. "I want this bitch to apologize to Mal. I want her offline. I don't want to see her open her dumb mouth again."

I shake my head. "It's worth your badge?"

He takes a long breath, and when his gaze meets mine again, red stains his eyes. Hurt and pain and anger clash together, and I catch a glimpse of the man I used to know and respect. "I wanted to… show her how it feels. To be hopeless, to lose what she's worked so hard for. To have one moment, one person, change everything."

Hazel's mouth pops open, and I shake my head slightly, and she closes it. I don't want her making it worse. He still has a gun pointed at her head, my gun at him, and one word—even if it's an apology—might set it all off.

"The offer still stands, Tyler." I use his first name, and as much as I hate to do it, I lower my weapon. "Keep your badge. Make your family money. Mal wouldn't want you behind bars."

He sniffs, and a tear falls from his eye and rolls into his beard. "This de-escalation shit? It won't work on me. I know what I'm in for. I knew it the second I stole her shit. Knew I was too far gone when I dumped the paint on the car. And I knew what I was in for when I stepped into this house."

His right trigger finger moves, and I dive for him. My body slams into his, and a gunshot pops through the air, along with an ear-piercing scream. We collide into the couch, toppling it on its side with a crunch that echoes against my ringing eardrums. My knee pushes into his wrist, flattening it against the wood floor. His grip loosens on the gun, and his other arm grapples for my weapon on my hip. My fist flies into his jaw with a force I never knew I was capable of. My knuckles throb as his body goes limp underneath my own.

The silence that follows takes me by the throat, making speech impossible as my eyes search for Hazel.

"H-Hazel?"

"Hunter?" Her head peeks from the other side of the upended couch. "Is he…?"

"I knocked him out. Are you hurt?"

"I… I don't think so." She pats at her body while I do a visual examination. The gunshot still rings in my ears, making the sirens in the distance feel like a hallucination.

Her hands slide down her side, and a small gasp slips through her lips. She pulls the fabric of her oversized hoodie, revealing a hole near her hip.

"Oh my—"

"Check your skin," I order, flipping Weir onto his stomach to cuff him. As soon as he's restrained, I push to my feet and get to her side. She's lifted her hoodie, and I see a slight graze, but nothing that requires stitches, I don't think. Relief rushes over me, and I can't help but pull her into my body, feel her against me.

Her arms wrap around me, and she shakes against my vest. "How… how did you…?"

"You'll have to thank some very dedicated followers." I hold her tighter, not giving a damn about the fact that she's streaming right now, that I shouldn't be doing this, that this place will be swarmed with patrol guys in under a minute. "Your pocket recorded the whole thing."

She jerks, fumbling for her phone. "I… I completely forgot I was even…"

"Might want to let them know you're okay." I give her a half grin, relief swamping me in a joy I haven't felt in a long time. The pendulum swung so far to the panic and fear that it's diving into the extreme of the opposite emotions, and I grab her by the cheeks and plant a kiss on her lips before I have time to talk myself out of it. "You… You are okay, right?" I ask, holding her close, resting my forehead against hers.

"I'm okay." She rises on her tiptoes and gives me a sweet peck on the lips. "I mean, I'm not, but I'm safe."

The sirens grow louder in my ears. I press kisses to her forehead, to her cheeks, her nose, her chin, then hold her close. Having her safe is just fine for right now.

chapter twelve

Hazel

The next week goes by in a flurry of police and media interviews. The fact that the whole thing was live made it all a media-fest, and I ended up with sponsorships and donations and realized just how awesome the world can be.

I don't deserve any of it.

Even though Hunter explained that Mal's business was shut down from the health department and not me, I still have this relentless pang of guilt piercing my stomach every time I think of it. I've gone cold turkey on gaming and streaming for the moment—despite getting all new equipment—the shame and sorrow so consuming I can't pretend it isn't destroying me.

How could I be so flippant with my remarks? I'm someone who puts myself out there all the time, opens myself up for the hate, however undeserved, and then I go and do it to someone else? No matter how bad the café was, it wasn't my place to vent about it to thousands of people.

I debated on what to do all week. Hunter said I didn't owe anyone anything, that I was the victim. I appreciate his protectiveness and support, but there was more than one victim in this.

The weather has turned from a breezy, bitter October to chilly November, and I crunch through a pathway of frozen, fallen leaves to a red door. I raise a gloved finger and press the doorbell, the familiar song of the Amazon Ring playing out into the crisp air.

A muffled voice comes over the doorbell. "What are you doing here?"

I nibble on my bottom lip and pray my voice comes out strong and unwavering. "Mal?"

"Yes. If you're here to gloat or give me money or make yourself feel better, don't waste your breath."

My heart sinks for her, the crack in her voice reaching through the intercom and slapping me in the face. "I… I'm not here for any of that."

"Then what do you want?"

I lean over, meeting the video camera with my eyes. "I'm sorry," I say with no preamble. It's what I came here for, what I need her to know. "I'm sorry for what I said about your café. I exaggerated, I made a joke out of it, and I was wrong."

She doesn't respond, and after a moment, I straighten

and take a deep breath. It's okay if she doesn't forgive me; I didn't expect her to. It's okay if she hates me. It's okay if she thinks this is just an attempt to save my reputation, or another way I can make a spectacle out of her, or if she thinks it's a publicity stunt. She can think all of those things, and I wouldn't blame her.

I step off the porch, and when I get to the end of the walk, I hear the door open behind me. For a moment, I imagine a gun pointed at my head—a recurring nightmare I've had all week—but it's just a short, cute brunette woman in jeans and a sweater. Her hair is curled, bouncing over her shoulders. A frown is set on her face, but from what I can recall, she had a beautiful smile. It was so big that it pushed her cheeks up into her eyes.

She crosses her arms and leans against the doorframe. "I'm sorry, too," she calls out, just loud enough for me to hear. "I didn't ask my husband to do what he did."

I stuff my hands into my coat pocket. "I know."

She nods, and a silent understanding passes between us before she shuts the door, and I get into my car. I drive to the nearest 7-Eleven, the weight of guilt already lifting from my shoulders.

chapter thirteen

Hunter

…this case will be closed, and charges have been accepted through the district attorney's office.

I put my name on the bottom and hit send, officially closing Hazel's case. A deep sigh drops from my lips, and I slump in my chair, refusing to let my gaze drift to the empty desk across from mine. I'll never understand the mindset of some people—to seek their own justice toward the people they blame. Hell, the anger that surges through my bloodstream at the image of Weir pointing that gun was enough to set the world on fire, yet I didn't break any law to stop him. And I'm not going to break any law to show him exactly how I feel about it, either.

I rub at my jaw, wishing I could get rid of the sick taste of betrayal, but I know it'll take a while. At least I have something to look forward to—as soon as I'm off, I'm heading directly to Hazel's place to ask her on an official date.

An IM pops up on my computer, Cooke's name in bright blue.

You at your desk?

Yep.

Not a minute later, the thump of Cooke's booted feet hit the hallway outside my glass case office. His wide frame fills the doorway, his thumbs hooked into his duty belt. The overhead light reflects off his bald head, his lips in his signature flat line. The guy looks intimidating as hell, but he's a teddy bear with a beard.

"Sarg," I greet with a nod.

He takes a step inside my office, his eyes flicking to Weir's empty desk before coming back to me. "Never did tell you good work on that burg case."

I let out a hollow laugh. "Wish I could say I'm proud of it."

"Don't know why you aren't." He leans his back against the wall, his gear clinking against the plated glass. "Usually these cases go unsolved."

I tap my finger against the edge of my desk, shaking my head. "I arrested a friend. A fellow officer. A brother." The ache in my heart leaks into my voice, and I hate myself for it.

Cooke's quiet for a beat, then his heavy footsteps cross the room. Weir's chair creaks under the unfamiliar weight. "You know what's better than catching a bad guy? Catching a bad cop."

The ache in my chest grows, and I clench my fist to keep myself from rubbing at the spot. "Guess I'd like to think there aren't any of those."

"That's naïve, and you know it. Don't be a dipshit."

That cracks me, and the unexpected laughter alleviates some of the pain.

"Look, it sucks having to arrest one of our own. There's a bunch of emotions that come with it. So, if you need someone to talk to—"

"Aww, Sarg," I tease. It's getting a little too heavy in here.

"I meant a therapist, dummy. I ain't qualified for that shit." He pushes from his chair and digs into his front pocket. "And don't get too comfortable in that seat."

He hands me a folded paper, and I furrow my brow at his knowing expression. He gives me a nod and then leaves without another word.

I check the hallway after him, but most people are avoiding my office. Either they don't know what to say or they don't want to seem too curious. Either way, the silence isn't too bad right now.

I unfold the paper, my stomach leaping when I see what's printed there.

To Whom it May Concern,

I recommend Detective Hunter Stoll for a position on the Major Crimes team, as well as Officer of the Year...

He lists my qualifications, and I'm humbled and stunned to see a list of more than just Hazel's case. For years, I felt like I was completely unnoticed, closing cases and paying my dues. Turns out someone did notice… and respected it. Maybe even more than I did.

The corner of my lip twitches, and I tuck the letter of recommendation into my top drawer.

chapter fourteen

Hazel

I shut down my computer and stretch my back. That was a long stream, even for me, but I felt like I needed to make up for the weeks I went MIA—a few by force and few by choice.

My shoulders drop, and I let out a long exhale, stroking Cheeto in my lap. It feels good to be back. Hopefully some normalcy will enter my life after the whirlwind.

The doorbell rings, and my knees crack as I push from my desk chair and lock up my game room. I check the newly installed camera I put on the doorstep as I make my way there. I only see the top of the man's head as he shifts his weight from left to right leg, but I'd recognize that gorgeous hair anywhere.

"Hello, Detective," I say as I swing the door open. He's a vision in casual clothing—jeans that hug his magnificent ass and a dark hoodie that I guarantee leaves with a pound of orange cat fur on it.

"Hello," he says, his breath fogging up into the crisp air. I stand back to let him inside, waving him forward, but he shakes his head. "I… Well, I wanted to tell you officially. Your case has been closed."

I raise a brow, my heart thumping hard and fast. I beg my feet not to tear me from my spot and bring me into his arms.

"About time," I tease, and a nervous laugh falls from his lips.

"I'm not great with paperwork." He scratches his scruff. "I put that off till the very end."

"You'd think you'd speed that up a bit. Considering." I cross my arms and rest against my doorframe.

"I did. There was a lot."

I bite away a grin, imagining him typing the report like a madman. I kinda hope he dashed over here the second he closed it.

"So… you had to let me know in person because…?" I pry playfully. If he needs a push, I'll give it to him.

He lets out a shaky laugh, and he meets my eyes with those seagreens I hope I get to see on the daily. "Give me two seconds." He pulls his phone out and taps a few things on the screen. Then he slides it into his pocket. "I'm clocked out, no longer the detective on the case…" He spreads his arms. "So… how 'bout it?"

I snort. "How 'bout what?" If he thinks he's getting

away without asking me, he better think again.

His arms fall. "Uh… you? Me?"

"Hunter…" I tut at him. "You're smoother than this."

"Not really."

My shoulders shake with silent laughter. "Well, try. I've been thinking about this for a while now."

"And I'm blowing it."

"A little."

He runs a hand through that fantastic hair. "Hazel, would you like to go ou—"

My feet no longer behave themselves, and I close the distance between us in a nanosecond. My lips find his, and his hands find my waist, and my breasts find his chest, and our tongues find each other, and next thing I know I'm dragging him inside and slamming him against my door, closing it with a bang.

"I cleaned my room," I tell him between kisses, reaching for the hem of his hoodie. My body can't take much more of the distance I've put between it and his, and I'm dying to see what's underneath that uniform.

He laughs around our kisses, allowing me to strip his hoodie off and toss it away. He takes my face in his hands, cradling me like a treasure, and I didn't realize how sweet he was going to be, so I pull back on my attack… just a little.

"Not saying I don't want to do this," he says, resting his forehead against mine, "but I need to know this isn't a fling for you."

"What?"

"When we talked about this before… you worried I would sleep with you and disappear."

"I was just joking."

The corner of his mouth lifts, and he presses a sweet kiss to the tip of my nose. "Were you?"

My heart stutters, and heat fills my cheeks. "Maybe… I don't know."

His hands drift from my cheeks, caressing my neck and then rubbing my shoulders. He looks me dead in the eye, and I try not to get distracted by his handsome features and pay attention to what he says.

"I don't do flings. I honestly haven't done much of anything for a long time. It's… not in my nature to get attached." He lets out a deep breath. "And sex is… intimate for me. Vulnerable. Not something I do lightly."

My heart practically sings. "You just made yourself ten thousand percent more attractive to me."

Red tinges his ears, and I tug on the sides of his t-shirt to pull him closer.

"What I'm saying is, you're important to me, Hazel. And… I want to be important to you."

I want to admit to him he's more important than he knows. I'd like to tell him we're completely twinning right now with the "long time" thing, that I haven't been with anyone since my divorce, that I don't give my heart away so easily, that I rarely have relationships outside of the internet.

But my lips and voice don't want to cooperate, and I push up on my tiptoes to give him a kiss. "Can I call you by your title?"

He jerks back a little. "You want to call me Detective?"

"No." I kiss him again. "I want to call you my boyfriend."

He lets out a laugh that could cure cancer. "Damn it, you scared me."

"What, why?"

"Thought you were a badge bunny in disguise."

"Nope. Just a dork who fell for the detective on her case."

"A very cute dork."

"At least I have that going for me."

He takes my face in his hands and kisses me again, spinning me around so my back is against the door. "Which way is your room again?"

I giggle and point in the direction. He nods, then hoists me into his arms and over his shoulder. I pat his glorious ass the entire way there.

To call my room clean would be generous, but I at least made the bed. He plops me down on it and immediately covers my body with his. His weight is like a fantasy come to life, and I soak in the feeling, breathe in his autumn leaf scent, and try not to giggle too much, but I'm too freaking excited.

I grapple for his belt, unhooking it with antsy fingers

and zero vision, since he's too busy loving my neck for me to look down. His kisses are flint and stone, sparking life into every nerve-ending in my body. I finally break past the barrier of his belt and jeans, sliding my hand across him. He sucks in a harsh breath, and my heart beats straight out of my chest. He thrusts into my grip, his kisses morphing into nibbles against my skin. I can't think, can't breathe, only wanting more and more of him and his touch.

"Naked, please," I gasp between breaths, and his weight disappears only for a moment while he strips his shirt. His pants are undone, thanks to my determined hands, and his erection stretches his blue boxer briefs, sucking whatever breath I had clean out of me.

"You too," he teases, amusement and pleasure dancing in his eyes. He offers his hand, and I take it. He pulls me to a sitting position. His fingers trickle down my ribs, curling under the hem of my shirt. Goosebumps cover every inch of my skin as he eases the material up and over my head. I'd like to say I'm not nervous as hell, but… I'm nervous as hell. It's been so long since I've been naked with a man outside of my cat, and my stomach ties in knots, anxious and scared at what he'll think.

His eyes drift over me, taking me in, and I do the same to distract myself from my nervous thoughts, studying the hair on his chest, the tan line from his uniform, the defined muscles of his arms… I have to remind myself I need oxygen when I start to black out.

"You have a tattoo," he says, and I blink out of my

haze.

"You too." I nod to the tattoo on his shoulder.

He brushes the pad of his thumb over my hip. "Half a heart?"

I frown. "Yeah. I should get it covered up."

He nods, not prodding or asking more, and I'm grateful. Now isn't the time to talk about my ex-husband or what that tattoo meant to me. Maybe I'll get it covered or attach the rest of the heart.

I reach for his, tracing my nail around the crescent shape. "Moon?"

He grins, then eases me to the mattress. He rests on his arm while drawing shapes on my stomach. "My siblings and I all got moon phases when Emerson turned eighteen. I'm the oldest, so I have the waxing crescent moon."

My chest bursts, and I'm grateful his tattoo has a meaning that won't destroy the moment between us. "That's sweet." I turn my head to the side and kiss his bicep. He strokes my hair with one hand while the other continues to drive me absolutely insane with shapes near my bellybutton. "Will I be able to meet these siblings?"

A brilliantly bright smile hits his lips. "One day, yes. I'd like that a lot."

My soul sings, my heart absolutely flying out of my chest and into his safe hands. I reach for the back of his head, pulling hard so his mouth descends on mine. Knowing just how important his family is to him, and that he wants to bring me into that world someday makes me want him as close as possible. I shimmy in his arms, struggling to get his pants down. After a minute, he growls, leaving my lips and shucking his pants. He reaches for mine, yanking them and my panties off in one fell swoop, and I thank my sense of style for donning lounge pants and going sans bra on work days.

He kisses a path up my inner thighs, and my body quivers with anticipation, flushing with heat. I feel him everywhere—my toes, my stomach, my arms, my neck, my lips… my head, my heart. A shiver starts from the point of contact of his tongue up to the crown of my head. My fingers attack, latching onto his hair and pulling him closer.

"I want… I want… you," I breathe, my vision blurred from stars and ecstasy.

"You have me." His voice is hot against my skin, and I pull at his arms, frantic to get him up and over me. He lets out a laugh at my impatience and sheaths himself before settling between my legs. His eyes connect with mine, and I grab his hips and yank him forward. Shock fills his expression before an immense dark pleasure crosses those seagreen irises. He kisses me all over, spreading fire through my body and igniting the room. He moves slowly and taking his sweet time, eliciting pleasure with every single stroke.

"I'm close," I tell him, a little embarrassed it's been three seconds, and I'm already bursting.

He quirks a grin, kissing me sweetly on the forehead. "Good."

Then he sets his hand between us, rubbing me into climax. I throw my head back, pressing it into the pillow. His hands grip my hips, holding me steady as I ride it out, and when I open my eyes, he's looking right back at me, pleasure deep in those intoxicating eyes. But there's something else entirely—something I only dreamed of seeing in those seagreens, and I find myself falling for him over and over and over again.

He loves on me for so long body melts into his, and he takes me to heaven and back at least three times.

On the fourth trip, he goes with me, grappling for my hand and intertwining our fingers. Sweat forms along his forehead, dripping from the tips of his hair, and I've never felt closer to anyone in my life.

He falls next to me, and I try to catch my breath, my limbs too useless to move an inch. We stare at the ceiling, and in unison, a breathy, "Wow," escapes us both. Then we laugh.

I roll into him, letting his arms wrap around me. I've always prided myself on my independence, on making a name for myself, for not needing anyone. But resting in his arms, I feel safer than ever, and that's a feeling I won't ever take for granted again.

epilogue

Hunter

"I warn you… It's gonna get ugly."

Hazel tucks into my arm and nods once. "I'm ready."

I laugh, then open the door to Miles' place. Hershey barks and rushes for the front door, sliding on the rug. He ignores me completely and goes for Hazel, who is already cooing at the chocolate lab.

"Who is such a cute and excited puppy, yes? What is your name, buddy? Lemme see…" She examines the collar while my brothers and Paxton round the corner. Each of them gives me that knowing look before turning their gazes to Hazel.

"She's here!" Ransom calls out, and a thundering of footsteps overhead signals my sisters' pending appearance.

"I'm here, too," I grumble, but Ransom waves me off, offering his hand to Hazel. "I'm Ransom. I'll repeat it multiple times tonight because a lot of names are about to be thrown at you."

She laughs, shaking his hand with one of hers while the other rubs Hershey's belly. "I appreciate that."

Paxton and Miles introduce themselves right as Sammie and Emerson walk in. Sammie pulls her into a giant hug, then drags her away to the game room—probably to show it off.

"So," Paxton says, watching the girls and the dog exit, "you invited her to Binge Sunday. Big step."

"She's important." I point a finger at Ransom. "So be nice."

"I'm a gentleman always!"

"I beg to differ," comes a voice from behind me. Joy is here—Ransom's best friend. I'd say she'd keep him in line, but they cause more trouble together.

Miles takes Joy's coat, then he gestures for us all to get to the game room. I guess Oakley and Evan aren't joining us today. They're the only other occasional Binge Sunday attendees. It started out as family only, but our family grew a lot when Mom and Dad split. Our friends stepped up, and we found out just how lucky we were.

I descend the stairs, the room already dark, the only light coming from the glow of the projector TV Ransom set up for Miles, Sammie, and Emerson when they moved in. Hazel is sandwiched between Sammie and Emerson, and they're all looking at something on Hazel's phone. They laugh together, each of them having their own unique sound, and I grin. I wouldn't mind hearing that combined laughter for the rest of my life.

"Am I not allowed to sit by my girlfriend?" I ask, waving my arm at the lack of space for me.

"You get her all the time." Emerson slides even closer to Hazel. "It's our turn."

Sammie nods, hugging Hazel's other side. Hazel shrugs, like she doesn't have control here, and then she pats the spot in front of her on the floor.

I let out a sigh and plop down in front of her. Her fingers tangle into my hair, and I change my mind. This is the best seat in the house.

"So… what are we watching?" Hazel asks as Miles, Paxton, Ransom, and Joy all take their spots. Miles grabs the remote and toggles over to Love it or List it.

"I won last week's bet, so it's my show this week."

Hazel tugs on my ears until I tilt my head back into her lap. "Is that how this works?"

"Yep. We siblings take bets on who is going to win our reality show of the week. Whoever wins the bet gets to pick the next watch."

"I see. What's your usual show?"

"Hell's Kitchen." I grin. "I'm a fan of Gordan."

"You just like all the yelling," Sammie jokes as Miles sets up the first episode and grabs his notebook. It's worn, the pages almost full. It's probably the seventh or eighth notebook we've been through for our reality binge bets.

"All right. Hunter… you going love it or list its for today?"

"List it." I always bet list it. Miles takes the other bets and goes to close the notebook.

"Wait… Do I get to bet?" Hazel asks, her eyes round and curious, matching Hershey, who is trying to climb into her lap by using me as a stepladder.

All my siblings look in my direction. It's my call; we all know it. Family only. There have been very few who even got an invite, and even less who participate in the bets. Even Joy and Paxton didn't get the betting privilege until a year or two into it.

Hazel senses the atmosphere and quickly stutters, "Oh… i-if it's family only—"

I reach up and grab her by the back of the neck, pulling her to meet my lips. We Spiderman kiss for a second, and I realize this woman is my whole world, and I want her a part of every single bit of it.

"Which way are you leaning, Hazel?" I ask when we part. "Love it or list it?"

She grins wide, then turns to Miles. "Oh, I'm absolutely going with love it."

***

Thank you for reading!

Want more? Check out Cassie Mae's Give me a Love Trope Series, starting with Miles and Val's story, Enemies to Lovers!

chapter one

Miles

I should've used a damn razor this morning.

My fingernails scrape through my overgrown beard, the sound grating against my ears in the quiet of Professor Young's classroom. The screen of my Chromebook has been on the same question for two minutes, six seconds, my vision blurring every time I turn to it.

I swallow hard, forcing my hand away from my beard. My fist clenches to the right of my laptop. My knuckles graze the cold, hard surface of the long table I share with about twenty others here in the back row.

Damn it, there's a ticking in my brain—an internal clock that won't shut the hell up. Tick, tick, tick… I'm running out of time. Time for this exam, time in this career, time on this earth… It's all the same right now, when time feels endless, yet there's still not enough of it.

My gaze darts around the room, my hand going for my beard yet again. Scratching, pulling, tugging, plucking… I won't need a razor after I'm done with it.

Professor Young sneezes from his desk at the front, the whiteboard gleaming with green and red art he did to "get into the Christmas spirit." As much as I appreciate the giant tree with red bulbs, it does not quiet the niggling voice in my head.

Oh, you'll fail this one. You can't pay attention long enough. You don't know what you're doing. Why try? No one in their right mind would give you a medical degree.

I inhale a shaky breath, and a flash of red catches my eye.

Val reclines in the first row, her long, brown hair twisted around a pen at the top of her head. She pushes her laptop to the side, the bright red COMPLETE printed across the screen.

Thirty-two times, now, she's finished her exam before everyone else.

It's pathetic I know that. More pathetic I keep on counting. My jaw ticks, and my exhale comes out in a growl. She turns in her seat so I can see her more directly, doodling nonsense in her yellow spiral notebook. Her head bops like she's listening to a song only she can hear, not a drop of sweat on her, even though this exam determines whether we pass or fail.

She's passing. I know it. She knows it. And it kills me she can take a test without any of the tics that plague me.

I look at my knee that's bouncing like it's enjoying a nice day at the trampoline park. Trevor, my desk mate, keeps throwing me the side-eye, annoyance clear in his grimace. I try to calm the leg down, but then my whole arm starts shaking.

I run a hand through my hair. My fingers come away sticky, and I quickly swipe the residue on my leg, making it bounce even more.

The anesthetic process can be divided into several steps. Which of the following demonstrates the desirable effect of the pre-medicating step in the anesthetic patient?

My vision blurs slightly as I select *A: Reduces patient stress and anxiety.* Then I overthink it for a solid two minutes.

Val shifts, dragging my gaze from my laptop to her. She sighs, like she's bored, and my back teeth clench and slide off each other. I should be used to it by now—her superiority in *everything.* All started in pre-K. I was showing off my skills on the monkey bars, being the only kid who could successfully get from one end to the other. Then this short, round, pink-cheeked girl ties her hair back and swings her way across first try. My jaw was in the playground woodchips. She laughed, said it wasn't hard, and skipped away.

I missed the next three monkey bar attempts.

Her eyes drift from her doodles to me, a smile pulling at the corner of her lips. I swallow hard and turn to my exam.

My brain starts on a journey about what I did today—a calming technique my therapist taught me.

Woke up.

Took Hershey for a walk.

Made breakfast smoothies for myself and my housemates—and sisters. Two banana slices for Emerson, three for Sammie. More peanut butter for myself and none for Emerson.

Blend on low.

I take a deep breath, my leg slowing its cadence, my fingers avoiding my beard.

Humane Society after smoothies. The drive was uneventful and quiet. Snow was piled along the sides of the road.

I said hello to all the animals up for adoption when I got into work. Brewster was on my first round—a loveable pit mix I was afraid would be at the shelter forever. When I saw the big sign that splayed the wonderful words I'M ADOPTED! I made a sound I only make around animals.

I pray to God none of my siblings find out I'm capable of… *squealing.*

My lips curl into a grin. I gave him all the attention—saying goodbye, really—and my knuckles relax, my leg no longer feels the need to dance on its own. My jaw loosens, my back teeth appreciating the lack of pressure.

Right as I answer the last question, Professor Young says, "Time. Ready or not, hit submit."

Some groans float around the room, but for the most

part, the class seems more relieved than anything. It's our last exam before Christmas break, and I sit up straight and stretch my back.

"Mr. Stoll, Miss Johnson…?" Professor Young says once everyone starts packing it up. "See me for a second before you take off."

Val catches my eyes and shrugs. If he suggests she tutor me, I'm quitting this career.

I stuff my laptop into my bag, trying not to feel horrible about my bouncing leg as Trevor leaves without a word. One would think with an undergraduate and three years of veterinary school under my belt, I'd be used to exams, but I still shake like an 8.5 earthquake every test.

Val's up front already—of course—and I trip my way down the stadium steps, pulling the strap of my laptop bag over my head. It yanks some strands clean from my scalp.

Val's lips purse together, probably reveling in my state of distress. Everything's so easy for her, while I claw my way to the top of everything.

Professor Young leans against his desk, resting his hands on top of his portly stomach. He gives us his signature grin underneath his hefty beard. He grows it out this time of year to play Santa, and his sweaters reflect just how much he enjoys Christmas. Today he's donning a Rudolph, complete with a light-up nose and bells hanging from the antlers.

"I'm sure you're both aware of the coveted internship

position to work with Dr. Goff."

Oh, I'm aware, all right. It's been *the* goal. Dr. Goff is the number one rated veterinarian in the state, and he takes his knowledge and skill and offers that up to one student, usually a fourth year. His program is a surefire way to get a license and start practicing right away.

I nod, my voice stuck somewhere between my throat and my tongue.

Val has a much more succinct response. "I think everyone knows Dr. Goff, Professor," she says through a laugh that puts my nerves on edge. Laughing after an exam is something I've never had the urge to do. I'm prone to run to the bathroom in case I need to extricate my morning smoothie.

Professor Young chuckles, his sweater jingling with the action. "Well, I've recommended you two for the spot."

I trip backward, grabbing onto the closest thing to me so I don't fall to my ass, which happens to be Professor Young's Rudolph antler, positioned perfectly around the guy's man boob.

I jerk right into Val, and I pray I didn't touch any part of her breast.

A musical laugh floats from her lips, and she steadies me. "Dr. Goff? Are you for real, Professor?"

Professor Young nods. "You're both at the top of the class—neck and neck, to be blunt. He only has one spot, but I wanted you to know how impressed I've been."

He hands us each a freshly printed piece of paper. The

first real smile I've had since walking into this classroom creases my lips as I read over the letter of recommendation.

"I've sent these to Dr. Goff, and he said he'll be popping in next semester to observe each of you. He'll make his selection at the end of the year."

"He's coming to watch us?" Val asks, then nudges me. "No pressure or anything."

She says it like it's a joke, but hell, it's no joke.

"Hmm…" is all I manage to get out.

Professor Young puts his hand on my shoulder. "No need to worry. Relax over the break. Celebrate this achievement."

"Yeah, okay…"

He nudges me like a father would a son, and that should make me feel better, but it doesn't. My dad hasn't given me an ounce of affection my entire life, so I don't know how to react when someone does.

We each thank him, then I walk from the classroom in a haze. It isn't until we step into the sunlight of the bright December afternoon that I remember Val is next to me.

"Here we go again," she teases, and my gaze drops.

She's still that short, round, pink-cheeked girl on the playground. Maybe only five-two, coming to my mid-chest. She pulls the pen from her hair, letting the strands cascade across her shoulders and flutter to her waist. There's such an ease about her.

It grinds against every single nerve I have.

"Meaning?" My voice has finally made a non-shaky appearance.

"Oh, just our little friendly competitions." She kicks a chunk of snow on the path, and it explodes into powder. "Science fair, class president, the librarian position…"

"All of which you won."

An evil grin pulls her lips. "Are you surrendering already?"

"Hell no."

"Good. I'd hate to think you *let* me win when I get the call from Dr. Goff." She wrinkles her nose playfully, then turns to the west parking lot while I head east. Damn it, if she's who I have to beat to get this internship, I have no chance.

chapter two

Val

"I'm home!" I shout at the top of my little lungs as I enter the condo I share with my brother, Logan. We've both learned to announce our entrances, having walked in on our frisky parents way more than we'd like to admit. I mean, it was *all over the house.* Like, yay, you love each other, but they had a room with a lock. We joked all the time that they didn't know how to use a deadbolt.

I jam out to Taylor Swift in my earbuds as I chuck my shoes into the hall closet and hang up my backpack. My mood can't be shaken by anything in this moment. I aced my midterm for sure, got top selection for that coveted internship, and… *and!* Miles Stoll walked me to the parking lot.

I do a jig, my ass dipping low as I turn the corner into the living room/kitchen area, full-out decorated with lights, garland, and snowmen figurines. Logan pulls the jug of milk from his lips, his cheeks puffed with the liquid, his brows rising at my sweet moves. I sing the next line of Taylor's *You Need to Calm Down* at the top of my lungs.

He swallows his swig of milk, capping it with a half grin. "Test went well, I take it?"

I nod, continuing to sing as I move to the fridge. Our kitchen isn't made for two, so I kinda trap him in there while I search for a celebration snack. He mumbles something I can't hear over my music, so I yank my left earbud out as I straighten.

"Huh?"

He hands me the milk to put in the fridge. I slide it next to mine in the door. We don't share—he likes one percent. Bleck.

"You up for a party tonight?"

I tilt my head, eyeing the piece of cheesecake I saved for this moment. "No date?"

"Was I supposed to find one?" he jokes. I huff as I grab my cheesecake and hipcheck the fridge shut. My brother is notorious for avoiding any and all relationships. He doesn't want to get married, doesn't want kids, doesn't want any of it, and whenever I prod him about it, he shuts me out.

I slide a fork from the silverware drawer and pop the top on my slice of chocolate Oreo. "You're gonna get an earful." Mom and Dad—mostly Dad—will drill him about taking his sister to a work party instead of a girlfriend. None of us even know if he has one; heaven knows he'd never tell us about her if he did.

Logan nods, rolling his eyes. He bumps me out of the way for a fork of his own, and I grudgingly share my treat with him. "So, you think you aced it?"

Ah, the change in subject. I'll oblige, since I'm a great twin and all. A wide grin wraps around my fork.

"Professor Young put me in for the internship!" I squeal with no prelude. Might as well get to the good stuff—I'm a dessert first kinda girl.

"Nice." He indulges me with a loud high five, the clap echoing in our tiny kitchen. He tosses his fork into the sink with a clink, then slides around me. My brow furrows as he rushes to his room just around the corner.

"O-kay," I say around a mouthful of cheesecake. "Didn't think we were done talking, but whatever."

He laughs as he comes back, carrying a giant, sparkly pink gift bag.

"Ooh." I rub my hands together, and he holds it out to me. "What's this?"

"Early Christmas," he lies through his teeth. My unemotional brother. "Just open it."

I rip into it, the crinkle of the tissue paper filling my heart. Presents are my love language… that and food.

My fingers tumble over soft material, and I squeak out a gleeful, "Eep!" as I pull the big stuffed pit bull from the bag. "He's adorable." I cuddle him to my chest, rubbing my cheek against the soft fluff. My dream dog, and my whole family knows it. One day I'll get one.

Logan's cheeks blossom red. He hates all the cheese, and I soak it up, laughing and grabbing him in a hug. He can be embarrassed all he wants.

"Ugh, get off!" He tries to wriggle from my grip, but I've always been the more determined of the two of us. I top it off with a kiss to his cheek, which he cringes from, then I finally let him go.

"Thank you." I boop the nose of my new furry friend. He'll be added to my collection upstairs. I have a stuffed animal obsession, and I know I should have grown out of it a long time ago, but oh well. If I can't have a real animal, I'll pretend for as long as possible.

"I almost don't want to tell you what it really means."

My fingers run over the stitching along the paws. "Huh?"

He lets out a giant sigh, shoving his hands into his jean pockets. His white t-shirt is way too loose on him. The guy is so skinny, which is so not fair he got those genes while I got the short and stocky ones. But I got the fun and quirky ones, too, so I'm not complaining too hard.

"You have to promise not to make a big deal about it."

I snort. "You know I can't do that." I reach out and pinch him. "What's with you?"

He does that sigh thing again, and my excitement meter kicks in overdrive. I'd try to calm it, but I can't. Again… I've had the *best* day, and I have a feeling it's about to get even better.

His eyes meet mine. We have the same coloring—dark, dark brown. It's the only thing we have that identifies us as biological siblings. He's tall, thin, blond hair… while I'm a whole five-one-and-three-quarters, round, dark brown hair. I try to suppress my smile, but it can't be helped. He has a surprise up his sleeve; I know it, and I want it.

"We go to the party first," he says strictly, reminding me in an instant of Mom, pointer finger out and all.

I nod, putting on as serious of an expression as I can.

His eyes drop to the stuffed pit in my hands. "He's waiting at the shelter."

My stomach lurches. "Wait… what?"

Redness fills his cheeks. "His name is Brewster. He's four years old. He's not purebred, but he's brown with a little white spot on hi—"

I leap into my brother's arms, knocking the words and wind right out of him. "You got me a dog?" I ask, tears welling in my eyes, my feet bouncing, making my head bunch up his shirt.

"I said not to make a big deal!"

"I'm not," I say through my wet voice, still bouncing, still hugging. A dog. *A dog.* Mom and Dad never let me have a dog. And I never had the guts to ask Logan if we could have one here. With school and his job and the fact we don't have a yard…

Gah, my twin brother knows me well. I bet he's had

this Christmas present planned for freaking ever.

"You love me," I say, squeezing him harder.

"No, I don't. Get off me."

"You love me so much."

He pushes at my arms, and I let him untangle me. I expect the red cheeks, but not the smile on his face. "We'll go get him after the party."

"Isn't the place closed?"

He nods. "I meant we'll get him tomorrow morning."

"First thing?"

"First thing."

I'm tempted to hug him again, but he puts his hands out, stopping me. "Please don't tell anyone."

I shake my head. "Don't want any of your co-workers to know you have such a big heart?"

"Exactly." He turns toward his room, calling over his shoulder. "It's casual dress. Starts in two hours."

"I love you, Logan!"

"Yeah, yeah."

I laugh at his retreating back, then spin around with my stuffed pit. This is officially better than any other day I've had on earth. It's about as close to my topmost fantasy as I can get right now.

Internship: check.

Best doggy in the world: check.

Love of my life: well, it's a work in progress.

Miles' handsome face fills my mind, and I let myself indulge in a daydream of him pushing a lock of hair behind my ear, leaning in with those full lips and pressing them to mine. Brewster is at our feet, Miles' hands on my hips…

I inhale deep and sigh blissfully. Oh, maybe one day. For now, I'm going to revel in the fantasies I have that *are* coming true. And that means I must prepare for a puppy.

Also by Cassie Mae

Sweet

Friday Night Alibi
You Can't Catch Me
Stage Kissed
Secret Catch

How To Series

How to Date a Nerd
How to Score a Band Geek
How to Hook a Bookworm

Frostville Series

The Princess and the Pizza Man
Southern Spinster

Sweet with Heat

Reasons I Fell for the Funny Fat Friend
Switched
The Real Thing

Troublemakers Series

I Knew You Were Trouble
Double Trouble
Asking for Trouble
Getting into Trouble (coming September 2023)
Save you the Trouble (coming 2024)
Here Comes Trouble (coming 2025)
The Art of Trouble (coming 2026)

Beds Series

King Sized Beds and Happy Trails
Beach Side Beds and Sandy Paths
Lonesome Beds and Bumpy Roads
True Love and Magic Tricks

Spicy

Unexpectedly You
Pillowtalk
Broken Records

Give Me a Love Trope Series

Man in Uniform
Enemies to Lovers
Brother's Best Friend
Fake Relationship
Friends to Lovers

Nerdy Thirties Series

Flirty Thirty
Missed Kiss
Maybe Baby
Make Lemonade

Love in New York Series

Master of the Meet Cute

The Pleasure Pact

Roadside Romance

The Date Dilemma

Join my ARC team for these books!

Southern Kicks
Stroke of Luck

About the Author

Cassie Mae is the author of a dozen or so books. Some of which became popular for their quirky titles, characters, and stories. She likes writing about nerds, geeks, the awkward, the fluffy, the short, the shy, the loud, the fun.

Since publishing her bestselling debut, Reasons I Fell for the Funny Fat Friend, she's published several titles with Penguin Random House and founded CookieLynn Publishing Services. She is represented by Sharon Pelletier at Dystel, Goderich, and Burret LLC. She has a favorite of all her book babies, but no, she won't tell you what it is. (Mainly because it changes depending on the day.)

Along with writing, Cassie likes to binge watch Parks and Recreation and enjoys every Harry Potter weekend. She likes kissing her hubby, but only if his facial hair is trimmed. She also likes cheesecake to a very obsessive degree.

You can stalk, talk, or send pictures of Luke Bryan to her on her Facebook page:
https://www.facebook.com/cassiemaeauthorpage

Sign up for Cassie Mae's newsletter
#booktok with Cassie Mae
Follow Cassie Mae on Amazon
Browse Cassie Mae Books on her Website
Join Cassie Mae's Awesome Nerds!

www.ingramcontent.com/pod-product-compliance
Lightning Source LLC
Chambersburg PA
CBHW061430160726
47995CB00003B/836